EVEN THE BIRDS GROW SILENT

ALEX NYE

Even the Birds Grow Silent
© Alex Nye 2021

Cover illustration: Graeme Clarke

Published by:
Fledgling Press Ltd.
1 Milton Rd West
Edinburgh
EH15 1LA

www.fledglingpress.co.uk

ISBN 978-1-912280-44-5

Printed and bound by:
Print on Demand Worldwide, Peterborough

For my husband, Joe, and my children,
Micah and Martha. Much love.

Author's Note

I completed the first draft of *Even the Birds Grow Silent* in January 2018. It did the rounds of literary agents with no success, as they felt that the idea of having death as a compassionate female protagonist being interviewed by the editor of a top lifestyle magazine was too bizarre. Luckily for me, Clare Cain at Fledgling Press is braver than most, and has given me the confidence to release it into the wild. Originally it comprised quite a few more chapters and stories, but I decided to cut it down to the few I thought worked best, under the 'less is more' policy. I hope you enjoy the variety and the tongue-in-cheek spirit in which they are meant.

Contents

Oh Death!

'My name is death, and none can excel
I'll open the gates to heaven or hell.'

'I'll lock their jaws so they can't talk
I'll fix their legs so they can't walk
Close their eyes so they can't see
This very hour you'll come with me.'

American Folk Song

Short Disclaimer

Many of the stories contained in this manuscript are part of an interview between Death, the Grim Reaper, or however you want to describe her, and Marcia Helen Sinclair, Chief Editor of *A Class Act Magazine*. During the course of this interview – unique in its conception – the Grim Reaper is at pains to reveal insights into the last moments of the lives of famous historical figures, artists, writers, singer-songwriters mainly, and ordinary individuals whose stories struck her as poignant or memorable in one way or another.

It is understood that Death has agreed to this interview in hopes of having the opportunity to put her side of the story, at last. She feels she gets a very bad press nowadays, and wants to make a clean breast of it.

She wishes to make it clear that she does mean well, although that may be a little hard for you to credit. Having always struggled with her role as the Grim Reaper, she is keen to set the record straight. She does not wish to be grim, but has worn the label now for so long, that it has, unfortunately, stuck.

The stories and anecdotes shared here are in no particular order of importance, and Death herself offers a disclaimer that she wishes in no way to offend any person, either living or dead.

Remember that these are only some of the dark tales she has chosen to relate. She asks that you read these carefully, and offers the hope that we shall avoid one another for a good while yet, but, until such time as we may meet again…

Yours truly
etcetera…

Vincent and a Wheatfield

'Well? What was he actually like? In the end, I mean?'

I look at her, Marcia Helen Sinclair, Chief Editor of *A Class Act Magazine*, keen for another story. We have chosen to meet in the rooms of a top end five star hotel in Edinburgh, where a young waiter serves us afternoon tea.

'I didn't know him personally, of course. Not until…' I hesitate.

'Until?'

I'm thinking, of course, of a wheatfield in *Auvers*, a murder of crows darkening the sky.

When I came across him he was already wounded, I tell Marcia. He was lying there, blood seeping from a bullet hole in his stomach, but there was no pistol by his side.

The plush hotel with its lavish setting recedes, and a quietness falls as I cast my spell. Marcia listens.

But I first came across him long before this, I tell her. Whenever his mood darkened I was forced to walk beside him.

I loved to watch him paint. I'd never seen anything quite like it. The pure frenzy. He dashed oils out of those tubes as if there was a never-ending supply of the stuff, and then cast down the empty container, twisted into contorted shapes. I couldn't take my eyes off him, the way he worked.

Strange paintings. The people of *Auvers* thought he

was mad. Some of them were quite fond of him, but no one rated his paintings very highly.

He was a gentle man: strange, tormented by the thought of his returning illness when he'd have another attack, and be found with blue paint bleeding from his lips and chin. He couldn't face another episode. Yet between the attacks, he was capable of such joy. Capturing the beautiful colours and textures he saw filled him with euphoria. It was his reason for living, as vital as the air he breathed. Without art, he was nothing. That's what he believed.

'What was he like to work with?' Marcia asks. 'Was he difficult at all? Talkative? Fiery? What did he talk about?'

I smile to myself. 'I wouldn't exactly say I worked with him. At least, I don't think he would have seen it that way. '

I never knew if he could really see me. His gaze would sweep over me.

I had begun to walk with him many times before this, when he carried his easel and satchel through the fields, or during those long dark days when he was incarcerated in the asylum.

They didn't incarcerate him there against his will, I tell Marcia, just for the record. He asked to be committed. He couldn't trust himself, and knew when he needed help.

But Saint-Rémy drove him madder than ever, watching the other inmates, their arms wrapped about themselves, rocking back and forth, tortured by God knows what demons inside their heads. He wanted only to be quiet and to paint. Sometimes they let him set up his easel in the gardens, where he'd capture the trees and the bushes with reckless brushstrokes, the sad-looking patients on the paths, their shoulders sagging with their unimaginable burden, the colour leached from their clothes and faces. He painted them as blank aspects, the walking wounded. They made him feel sad. He needed help, he knew that, but he didn't want to become like them.

The hospital sat among olives and cypress trees. The walls were bleached white by the sun, and the faded blue paint of the shutters flaked onto the patients below, so that they looked up, wondering. Was it snowing? Blue snow?

There were baked clay tiles on the roof. Cypresses twisted like dark spires, casting shade. Clouds of pink blossom peeped beyond the high walls, which Vincent would paint, of course.

Vincent was one of those whose lives are lived on the edge. He couldn't have painted like that otherwise. As he painted away in the Yellow House, or in the open air, where he would set up his easel like a tripod, I would peer over his shoulder and marvel. I couldn't believe others were blind to it, his talent. No one else had ever painted like that before, and I suppose when that's the case, it takes people by surprise and even longer to believe in its worth.

It was his brother, Theo, of course, who saw in him what others could not – and Theo's wife, Jo. Without his brother's small handouts to pay for oil and paint, we wouldn't have his paintings now. You can't paint with thin air. You need materials. And if you buy materials, you don't eat – if you're poor, that is.

So, two days before he died I was nearby, of course. He'd had suicidal musings in the hospital in Saint-Rémy, and couldn't face another episode.

Nowadays, there might have been a pill to help him deal with the condition, but not then.

He needed peace and quiet, not too much excitement, no alcohol, his brother had urged that, but Vincent liked a drink with his friends. He had a good sense of humour, a sense of mischief, they liked him in the bars. He had drinking companions he'd meet up with, and they'd share a glass or two in the evening. I know what attracted them, these types. They'd exonerate and confirm one another, their need to find some peace of mind in the bottom of an empty glass, under the red and green faded lantern light of the public rooms, the gaseous acidy kick of the absinthe being their goddess and their queen. Couldn't resist it. But it wasn't that which killed him in the end. He needed a quiet, healthy existence. But he was always tempted back to the bars eventually. Nothing wrong with that. Every man likes a quiet drink.

In *Auvers* he rented a small room above an inn. The family took to him, a quiet, gentle soul they thought him. His room was filled with canvases, propped up against the walls, crowding out the tiny space. All he had was a bed and a chair. He ate downstairs, went out after breakfast to produce another unacknowledged masterpiece. I was watching him by this point. I knew the time was near, and it fair broke my heart to follow him. He was young still, in his prime. I liked him.

He fell into drinking with two young lads who teased him when he was in a bad way. He was tolerant with them. He knew he cut a bizarre figure, moving about the streets and fields in his scruffy peasant's gown, wearing an old pair of boots when he wore any, his sunburned skin creased with paint residue that somehow found its way into his flesh, and never found its way out again. The paint was in his soul, alright. He even tried to eat it once, did you know that? In one of his terrible episodes.

But now he appeared fairly lucid, calm. He was in love with life and art. If anything, he lived life too intensely. He was utterly driven, compelled to translate everything he saw into art. As far as Vincent was concerned, this world sang and pulsed with energy, and he wanted to capture every bit of it, convey that energy, share it.

Of course, the downside of being so attuned to the miraculous is that you also know the reverse – the darkness. Vincent knew the sickness would return. The acid-green sickness, the pulsating dull red of despair, the exhausting yellow sting of pain, too bright to be borne. He couldn't bear the thought of enduring it again. But he *would* have borne it, if he could.

I saw him standing there, the easel in front of him, and crept close through the rustling wheat stalks. The crop stirred and rippled in a faint breeze, but for me it did not move. I passed through it soundlessly. Like a wind.

Vincent was staring at the view before him, but there was something odd about his manner. He wasn't painting, for a start. His arms hung limp by his sides. He gazed, without moving.

I was always curious to see what Vincent would

paint next, so I stood behind him to examine his canvas.

'And what did you see?' Marcia asks.

Nothing. Blank as milk. Not a single mark on it. That alarmed me.

Then he turned his head sideways, almost as if he saw me. He picked up the easel, and with a violent gesture flung it sideways. It crashed to the ground against a haystack, and there it remained.

At the same time a murder of crows lifted up from the wheatfield before us and wheeled in the sky, like harbingers of doom. They hung there, inkspots against the sky, disturbed by the clatter of his broken easel.

The ability to paint left him just as suddenly as it had arrived.

It was maybe an hour later, perhaps two, that two boys arrived on the scene. It is difficult to tell. Time concertinas so. It implodes or stretches.

They came upon him sitting all alone among the wheat, his head in his hands, and shouted out his name.

'Eh? Vincent?'

One of them brandished a pistol.

Vincent did not respond.

'We've come to scare the crows,' the boy hollered, 'but it looks like you scared them first.'

'Yes,' the other cried. 'Vincent the scarecrow!' and they both began to laugh.

He half-laughed with them, tolerant, mild as ever. Vincent was the resident clown in *Auvers*. The madman, the fool, the stranger without a permanent address who dresses like a tramp and has few friends, although everyone knows him.

They were laughing, teasing, having fun at his expense when the pistol discharged accidentally.

One of them cursed.

'Idiot!' he cried, while the other paled in horror at what he'd done, staring at the pistol as if it was a poisonous snake with a life of its own.

Vincent crumpled.

I looked into the anguished eyes of the one with the weapon, and he looked back at me briefly. He dropped the pistol and knelt towards the body of the painter. But the other one pulled him away.

'Come on,' he hissed. 'We have to go.'

Vincent looked at the boy, and waved him away.

But the boy wouldn't leave at first.

Vincent grabbed him by the shirt, one of those young fellows he'd been drinking with in the bar only the night before, and pulled him down beside him.

He whispered something in his ear.

'I wanted to die anyway.'

Then he released the boy, who scurried away after his friend, the wheat stalks parting for them. The air seemed to shiver with their fear. I watched them running, the wheatfield rippling with their progress.

They were white with terror, repentant already. I saw the horror in their eyes at what they had done.

So did Vincent.

I crouched beside him, and watched as his eyes slowly glazed over.

I sat there until the sun dipped towards the horizon.

It was my duty to release him, to ease him on his way.

But I couldn't do it.

I couldn't watch him leave this world.

No one knew him. He would die unrecognized, his paintings forgotten.

The evening light faded, and the ground began to cool.

Vincent stirred.

He groaned.

He opened his eyes.

I watched him sit upright, and struggle to stand.

Holding a hand to his stomach, he had sufficient strength to stumble away through the wheatfield, leaving that scene behind him. His easel lay against the haystack where he had flung it, half-broken, in his rage. The rooks were silent now.

He dragged himself back to his lodgings in the village.

The family were out looking for him. They were worried when he did not return for his supper.

Adeline ran to him as he entered the inn.

'Monsieur,' she cried. 'You do not look well.'

She was only a child. I glanced at her and was glad to note that she could not see me. I knew I would have no dealings with this healthy thirteen-year-old daughter of the innkeeper, Ravoux. She would die in her bed at a ripe old age, the sun and dust of *Auvers* in her eyes.

Monsieur Ravoux stared after Vincent, frowning.

'Is there a problem, Monsieur?'

Vincent did not look back at them, but used the wooden handrail to pull himself up the staircase.

'No, but I have...'

Unable to finish his sentence, he waved his hand, and continued on his way.

I stood with the innkeeper and his daughter in the downstairs room as they listened to the door of Vincent's humble little room closing behind him.

Neither of them saw me.

Vincent lay down on the narrow bunk, surrounded by his canvases, and held his stomach where the red stain bloomed on his shirt.

He groaned intermittently and began to develop a fever.

I waited with him through the long dark night, and I was there when Monsieur Ravoux rushed into his room, having heard the noise from below.

Adeline ran to fetch the doctor, and sent off a telegram to Theo.

I stood like a ghost in a corner of the room, unobserved by the others. A pale witness.

Vincent, I knew, was thinking of the two teenagers who'd fired the shot. He was anxious they should not be blamed. He knew what would happen to them if they were accused. It would be the long drop for them, the noose around their young necks.

His doctor, Gachet, arrived and dressed the wound.

'What were you doing to yourself, eh, Vincent?'

'I tried to kill myself,' he murmured, making a huge effort to speak with clarity.

The doctor looked at him with that air of disappointment and pessimism he always wore, and which Vincent captured so accurately in his portrait of the man.

'I have failed even in that,' Vincent said.

Doctor Gachet glanced around at the canvases turned against the walls. Those facing outwards were bright and bountiful with colour, with thick texture. The doctor looked at them then shook his head.

Adeline and her father were nearby.

'There is nothing I can do for him,' Gachet murmured sadly.

Then he glanced back at the poor painter lying in his bed, the thin sheets tumbled about his legs.

'I have done everything I can,' he sighed. 'I have failed too.'

Theo arrived, and sat with his brother until he slipped into a coma.

'Do not accuse anyone,' he whispered, as Theo held his hand. 'I wanted to die. It was me.'

'No one blames you,' Theo murmured, trying to keep his voice steady. 'You have suffered too much. We will make sure you get better.'

Vincent looked at him and sighed.

'This sadness will never get better. It will last forever.'

He never spoke again. Hours passed, and Vincent became unconscious before he finally slipped away.

When I last looked, Theo was weeping over the empty body, but Vincent wasn't there anymore. He had moved to join me in the corner, looking back at the dishevelled and desolate little room, with its plethora of canvases which the great painter was now forced to leave behind.

I wondered at first how he would cope with that. Leaving his paintings.

'And how did he cope?' asks Marcia, who has been listening all this while.

I shrug.

He had to let go. They meant nothing to him anymore. They were just the remains. You see, what I cannot fail to notice in my years in this profession is that every person leaves behind traces of themselves: hair, dust, paper, trash, shoes, paintings, teeth. Graveyards are stacked with your broken bones. Cemeteries are landfill sites, overflowing with layer upon layer of forgotten decay, refuse, cast-off stuff no longer useful or wanted, because it no longer functions properly or serves a purpose. The valves no longer open and shut, the organs no longer pump and throb. The machine is abandoned. What is left is furniture, bricks, unpaid bills, bric-a-brac to be auctioned off, a mattress to be fumigated and washed free of stains. Memories which may or may not be passed down through the generations. If not, then they curl away like mist, evaporate on sea-filled air, disappear into the fog of life.

A tumble of unwanted possessions that no one knows what to do with anymore. That is all Vincent's paintings had become. Flotsam, left behind on the tide of life. They were pushed away in attics, chicken coops, mouldering basements, except for those his brother Theo managed to rescue... but it wasn't long before I had to escort Theo to the other side too. He had a troubling cough. He was a consumptive. He survived his brother by less than a year, then poor Jo, his widow, was left to shoulder the burden of what would happen to Vincent's art, which she did, admirably. He sold one painting in his lifetime, but she ensured Vincent's paintings were not forgotten.

Marcia has fallen silent.

She hasn't touched her tea, cooling in its cup.

'You've made me feel very sad, all of a sudden,' she admits, glancing down at the little screen of her phone which is patiently recording us.

'Yes, I'm sorry about that, but I suppose it is a sad subject.'

She concedes that it is.

Death Visits a Perthshire Wood

1953. Catriona and her brother Robbie.

They lived on an estate in Perthshire, where their father was gamekeeper.

Very close. Went about together everywhere.

Catriona was the youngest and idolized her big brother. Adored him.

They were both in high school at this stage. They caught the bus together, and when Catriona was bullied by the older kids, Robbie protected her. Got himself into a fight because of it, but he didn't care because he loved his little sister, would not suffer anyone to hurt her.

It wasn't a particularly happy marriage between the parents, as far as I can recall. A bit of an atmosphere, although I never really got to the bottom of what that was all about. I so rarely do, you see.

They lived in an old house with crow-stepped gable windows, and a view onto fields and woodland, a soft purple haze on the horizon. I remember it so well, because it was my favourite season, autumn. There was a faint smell of woodsmoke on the air, and a grey mist uncurling from the treetops.

All day I'd been enjoying the woodland, listening to the murmur of the nearby burn, gazing into its copper-bottomed water, wondering what to expect. The earth was a tangle of twisted roots and moss-clogged runnels. I pushed my way through the ferns, burrs sticking to my clothes. Everywhere was the smell of mint and thyme, ragwort and nettles. I breathed deeply and took in the smell of rich minerals, moss and decay. Oh, how I love that smell of decay. Rich fungi creeping underground where no one sees it, until it pushes its way to the surface or explodes from the hollow of a rotting tree-trunk. Stunning to look at, with its frilled edges, soft gills all bone white and murderous.

I had no idea who I was there for. I'd been called to attend the gamekeeper's house. There were four of them in all, and two of them weren't at home: the children.

Just the parents, then.

There was an ominous atmosphere between the adults, but at the same time the woodland was peaceful. Why would this rural idyll be targeted today of all days, when the sun climbed the dip in the valley, and shone its misty benevolence on all the land beneath?

I had no idea.

As I said before, I don't always know who I'm coming for when I arrive on the scene.

Like a war photographer in a conflict zone, I simply have a job to do, a task to perform. I am called upon to be professional, and this is what I strive to be, at all times. Imagine if Death gave a sloppy performance? That would not do at all.

In the kitchen the parents were arguing. Not so much violently, but with a quiet, passive aggression. She slammed the kettle onto the stove with a deliberate clatter, as if to make a point. A show of rebellion, perhaps.

He merely looked at her, and went out.

With his gun.

I followed him down to the paddock, dogged his footsteps, wondering now and again if he would glimpse me out of the corner of his eye.

I saw him lift his head to the trees where I stood. I held my breath, but his gaze left me and he turned away.

I looked up into the canopy, layer upon layer of beech and larch, chestnut and oak, crimson and gold.

A pheasant exploded from the undergrowth with a wild clatter, and others followed, flying low across the slope of the hillside, within his aim.

He lifted his rifle, held it there against his shoulder, following the movement of their flight.

They were clear within his sights, but he lowered his gun, and they squawked on into the far woods, to live another day.

It wasn't his job to shoot them. He was there to harvest them for the season, so that Mr Kendrick who owned the land could invite his guests for some sport.

I felt his anger as he stood there in the lower paddock, leaning against the gate. All this land and none of it his, yet it existed in his blood. It belonged to him. No one else could claim that connection with the forests and woodland, the sloping hills and valleys, the wildlife. He knew it inside out, since he was a boy.

I admired that, and I connected with it.

I have always been a great lover of Nature, you might be surprised to know. I'm an outdoors kind of girl, and this peaceful Perthshire wood was pure delight. Wispy grey smoke, lilac mist, soft mellow shadings of trees in the distance. Like a fifteenth century tapestry, blurred gold by distance.

It was hard to credit there was dissonance here, instead of harmony. Human beings bring their own stories to bear on the quiet landscapes around them.

It made a welcome change to be here.

I breathed in the scent of fungus and mould, minerals and moss which crept their way over the rocks, through the soil, and beneath the little stone bridge at the bottom of the lane.

I stood in the trees watching him, until he abandoned his post by the gate.

Then he trudged his way back up to the house, left his rifle in the front porch, and found his wife in the kitchen.

He took her in his arms, and kissed her.

That completely threw me.

In all their years of marriage, I think that must have been a first.

I left them there, and drifted off down the lane, where I could hear the children returning home from school.

Robbie, and his little sister, Catriona. Cat, for short, he always called her.

I could hear them coming, calling to each other, playing. He ran on ahead and she followed.

They slammed the glass door, but no one answered.

It seemed like there was no one at home.

Their father's gun was still propped in the porch where he'd left it.

They were used to rifles lying about the place. The one essential rule was that you broke the barrel, emptied it of bullets, and stored the ammunition separately. Their father never left a rifle loaded.

Robbie – who had a flair for dramatics – picked up the rifle.

I held my breath.

He rehearsed a perfect death scene, arms akimbo, body jerking with the impact of the bullets raining down on him, as he fell backwards onto the couch.

'I got me an Injun,' he shrieked, leaping up again, resurrected.

'Come on, Cat.'

He handed her the rifle.

'Blow me away!'

And she did.

There was silence afterwards.

A terrible silence.

It followed Cat all the rest of her days.

I went back there a month or two later, but the family had moved away to Canada by then. The house stood empty. It was one of those incidents which haunted me, left an itch, so I had to keep going back.

That beautiful soft undulating countryside, with smoky hillsides and the purple haze of woodland.

Cat hadn't realised she was such a good aim, and neither of them, of course, had realised the rifle was loaded. It was never loaded. Their father always kept the ammunition separate. He was strict about that.

Yes, that was a difficult case.

I came upon Cat many years later, when she was an old woman. She had children of her own by then, a grown-up family. But in her final moments, as the last breath left her body, it was her brother's name I heard on her lips.

Robbie.

Margery and Rita Hayworth

I visit households where no one is expecting me.

I knock on the door.

No one opens, but I enter anyway, slip into the air you breathe. The soft feminine breath of me enters your lungs, slides into your bloodstream, slowly begins to blossom like an invisible flower.

It was 1954. Margery was eleven years old. She sat in front of a mirror, practising her Rita Hayworth pout, her chestnut hair twisted back from her face in a maturely-crafted design. She had tossed her old doll aside, abandoning it in favour of more worldly accoutrements.

A tortoiseshell brush and comb, heavy-backed and solid, that once belonged to her grandmother – now deceased; a bright red lipstick rolling on the floor in the dust at her bare feet, uncapped. In her lap was a magazine which lay open at a picture of Rita herself, smouldering for the camera with her eyes ablaze.

Margery looked at the photo, and then looked at herself, and tried to copy that moody gaze.

She had never looked at herself in this way before.

Am I pretty? she asked herself.

Could I be glamorous and sophisticated when I grow up?

When will I grow up?

Am I anything at all like Rita Hayworth?

Margery was about to leave her childhood behind,

and with it, the cast off doll with its powder-blue frock and flouncy petticoats.

Margery was considering her future.

However, I am afraid to tell you the unfortunate and unpalatable truth that she had no future.

I was waiting in the wings, even then.

When she next looked in the mirror, she saw me over her shoulder. Usually, I have no reflection, but she could see my eyes, and she smiled. She smiled at me as if I were a friend, little suspecting I had come to rob her of her dreams. Most people are surprised when they find out I'm a woman, and I suppose to Margery, my eyes looked unthreateningly feminine, therefore posing no menace.

I don't know why you lot always expect a man.

'Margery, come down at once!' a voice shouted from downstairs.

At first Margery ignored the command, waited for it to repeat itself. She was in no mood to hurry, in no rush to leave her dreams of being Rita Hayworth behind.

'Do you hear me, Margery? Come down this instant!'

Margery hopped off her stool, grabbed her dressing-gown and hurried down the stairs.

I stayed behind in the room, gazing at the mirror in which Margery had gazed, and trying to see my own reflection.

Nothing.

Not. A. Thing.

I could hear the rumble of discontented voices downstairs. The mother scolding; Margery being a touch insolent perhaps, certainly not bothering to appease her nagging mother. Oh, how that woman could nag and how she would wish she'd held her tongue when morning came.

'Stop admiring yourself in that mirror,' I heard the mother say.

'Is that what she's bin doin?' A male voice joined in. 'Is that what she's bin wasting her time on?'

'Yes, and…'

The voices merged into one cacophony of sound, while Margery rose above it all, silently holding Rita Hayworth in her mind, and longing also for the abandoned doll in a sudden rush of love for what was past, for what she might be losing.

'… you mark my words… there'll be all hell to pay when…'

On and on it went.

Margery stopped listening.

1954 and she had the rest of her life before her. She was eleven years old. There were so many selves she had yet to become. She could reinvent herself over and over like a chameleon until she reached the final blueprint that satisfied her. She had no idea yet what that might be.

All she had was a glossy black and white picture of a Hollywood star who was old enough to be her mother.

But a mother very different from the one in the kitchen with the apron and the tired expression and the cigarette hanging from her swollen lip.

Margery did not want to aspire to be a domestic drudge leaning over a frothy sink, washing dishes, with a hundred small children mewling about her ankles. But she could aspire to be Rita Hayworth. That was certainly something worth striving for.

All she needed was a mirror, a lipstick and the ability to pout.

Margery went to bed that night feeling quite well. Her cheeks were a little flushed perhaps, but that was all.

What neither she nor her parents realised was that Margery's fresh young body had already begun to be harvested for decay. The virus lay hidden, dormant inside her, ready to fructify and multiply in a manner that would be beautiful if captured under a microscope.

In the morning Margery did not get up for school.

The mother shouted herself hoarse, and finally, in despair, came up to investigate.

The mirror was still there, propped against the wall, with the uncapped lipstick beside it, the heavy brush and comb set that had once belonged to Margery's grandmother, and the magazine. The doll was tucked in (courtesy of *Yours Truly*) beside Margery, who was hot and sweating and covered with painful-looking pink and white pustules which all but disfigured her face.

She was crusted with them, even her eyelids and her ears. Her eyes would not open for the yellow pus congealed there, her throat so sore she could not speak.

Her mother cried out, sank to her knees.

In those days, you see, there was no vaccination for measles. Diseases came and went, and children endured them, but some cases were so virulent that children died. Fresh young blood, cut down where they played in the fields of their imagination.

Margery's face was no longer pretty, and no longer resembled the glamorous visage of Rita Hayworth.

It pains me to say it, but say it I must.

The flourishing of decay is as natural, as seductive to me as the flowering of a meadow. I cannot resist it. I observe its development with a professionally detached interest and a slightly shameful fascination. The rash encrusts a lithe young body, and wreaks its external havoc, leaving it raw, crimson, inflamed.

The mother did not scold.

She had no telephone so she sent her youngest child for the doctor.

There was nothing he could do.

Plenty of liquids, keep her temperature down, wait for the disease to run its course, and see who would win the battle for her body in the end.

Margery was in quarantine.

Her younger brothers and sisters were sent away.

The angry mother nursed her child, but to no avail.

After the funeral, which took place in the rain a few weeks later, the mother sat downstairs in the kitchen with her apron over her head, paralysed with grief.

Life would go on. It always does.

She heard heavy footsteps stealthily climbing the stairs – Margery's father, ashamed to give in to his grief.

The mother stared at the ceiling. Her kitchen was directly below Margery's tiny bedroom.

The ceiling creaked again.

In Margery's room the father picked up a copy of a magazine left lying on the floor, shoved behind the mirror. Hollywood stars, that kind of thing. Something he'd never encouraged.

It flopped open at a picture of Rita Hayworth. He sat on the stool and put his head in his hands.

I watched all of this.

I took note.

Human beings.

They live and they die by the smallest of increments.

And I am their only witness.

Tusitala, Teller of Tales

He was never a well man, you know.

I think of him coughing in his narrow cot as a child.

Many was the time when I had to stand all night long beside his bed in case of an emergency, listening patiently as he wheezed and croaked his way towards another dawn. It was a wonder he survived at all.

I think of him in that damp house in Inverleith Terrace, before his parents moved to the more salubrious Heriot Row where the air was purer.

But the damage was already done by then. The damp had got into his chest, and it remained with him for the rest of his life. So I dogged his footsteps, appearing as his health deteriorated, receding again when it looked like a false alarm. I began to think he would live forever, in spite of his cough. Not that I begrudged him that, of course. I'm just glad he lived long enough to write his books. What would the world be like without *Treasure Island*, or *Jekyll and Hyde*?

It would be a poorer world indeed. So, I was summoned to his bedside, and arrived to find a small ailing boy, weak, pale, pitifully thin, who looked set not to last till morning. The mother had a weak chest too. It ran in the family.

I stood at the window, outlined against the moonlight. The boy opened his eyes and looked straight at me. He recognized me alright, I could tell.

He gave me a look.

'*Go away,*' he said loudly. '*I have too much living to do.*'

I did a double take at that. Saw me, plain as day.

That look of his became familiar over the years, as he continued to elude me, cheating me of the final prize you must all surrender in the end. I'd arrive to find him on his last legs, coughing his way to the grave, only to leave empty-handed. He was desperate to hang onto life. There were things he wanted to do. He didn't want to be a sick, ailing boy, confined and bedridden. He wanted to travel, see the world and write stories.

The father – as you know – was a lighthouse engineer, and rather hoped that if his son survived, he would follow in the family tradition. But engineering didn't appeal to Robert. He was happy to travel with his father around the islands, sailing to Orkney and Shetland, brave the rough seas and observe the rugged coastline, but only to glean inspiration for his stories, not to learn about structural engineering. He admired the towers his forebears built, their incredible ability to withstand the onslaught of tide and storms for centuries on end – they are still standing even now, as testimony to his father's skill and ingenuity. He was proud of the fact they helped save thousands of lives, that the light shone out from those beacons like a symbolic ray of hope against the storms of darkness. Robert felt as if his father and grandfather were cheating death, defying the odds, robbing *Yours Truly*, I suppose, of booty.

I didn't mind.

I always appreciate and applaud the efforts of humankind to save one another and avoid my maw if at all possible. Why would you not? It's part of your DNA. Even the scurrying spider runs from the heel that would crush it, and hides in the murky shadows till the danger is passed.

I imagine you may wince slightly at the image of a revolting eight-legged creature feigning stillness behind a chair leg, before getting ready to run like hell, all of its eight legs rippling and jointing at the same time. That ought to be the least of your worries. The horrors I have seen are unimaginable.

Robert loved the sea. He absorbed the stories of smugglers and wreckers, those shady creatures who would listen to the cries of drowning men, having led their boats onto the rocks with a swaying lantern, before reaping the spoils washed up on the tide.

The young boy would forget to listen to his father's instruction, and listen instead to the wild wash of the waves. Maths wasn't really his thing, so instead he would invent his own stories.

The lighthouses his forebears built cheated me of bodies to harvest, while young Robert himself tantalized me with his offering, only to pull back again at the last. I am not one of your rough pickings, he seemed to cry. Oh yes, he and I were on familiar terms.

He would rise, leave the bedroom, recover his health long enough to live another day, another year, well into his adulthood, strong at last although plagued by a persistent cough. But he never forgot the dark figure who stood over his childhood bed, watching.

He knew who I was, alright.

And he loved life enough to cling onto it, to wring the very last drop of adventure and creativity out of it before he would give in, and submit himself, at last, into my care. He did not want my arms around him. He wanted to live.

When a journalist, like you, Marcia, asks me what my defining memory of him is, I know exactly which one to select.

Immediately I am transported to a rocky gully beside the River Allan, where the beech trees grew tall and made secretive hollows of the woodland. The river gushed along a deep gorge with steep sides. Watery tributaries broke off and cut a path through the bedrock of stone: a narrow gully smelling of wild garlic, where Robert hid during a woodland walk and told himself stories. He found a spot in a low mossy cave which afforded some shelter, and it was here he pulled out a small wooden stool, his pen and his folded pages, and began to write, surrounded by the tumble and cascade of water. Rainwater dripped from the lip of the cave, and green ferns curled against the light.

I came across him here, and this time he did not even notice me. His head was bent and all I could hear, apart from the murmur of the Allan Water, was the feverish scratching of his quill. I peered over his shoulder and watched him write.

It was a special moment.

I will begin the story of my adventures with a certain morning early in the month of June, in the year of grace 1751, when I took the key for the last time out of the door of my father's house.

I didn't know it at the time – and neither did he – but this ink-stained and watermarked manuscript would become *Kidnapped*.

I could have taken him at any time. He coughed into his handkerchief even as he worked, but – and I am loathe to admit it – I did not want to deprive the world of his stories. If I could hold off a little longer, then I would. I crept away from that mossy cave and let him be.

When I next came across him, it was some years later at his home on the South Pacific island of Samoa. He'd built his own house by then, *Vailima*, and made friends with the locals. They called him *Tusitala*, Teller of Tales.

He sat or stood on the high veranda, surrounded by virgin forest, listening to the elaborate bird cries, enjoying the feeling of paradise and wilderness. His failing health meant he couldn't return to Scotland now, even if he wanted to. He would never have survived the journey and he was happy here, with his wife and two step-children. The natives were his friends and he spun his tales from this position of privileged isolation. Sometimes he would find himself bedbound and I'd arrive to find him lying prone in a hammock, swinging gently, or propped up on pillows, his white face beaded with sweat and his eyes dark with lethargy. He would glare at me angrily, and turn his back on me.

Then I would be glad to leave and watch from a distance as he enjoyed a return to his old furious energy. His appetite for life and adventure was immense. He sailed in canoes, he climbed mountains, he braved the high seas: he wrote and he wrote.

'I wish to die in my boots,' I heard him say. 'No more Land of Counterpane for me. To be drowned, to be shot, to be thrown from a horse – aye, to be hanged, rather than pass again through that slow dissolution.'

I waited until his best works were behind him before I could be persuaded to carry him away. As it happens, the end was very sudden.

He woke on the morning in question with a desire to go for a long walk in the forest, to take the sea air, and spend the afternoon writing. I followed him that day, kept my distance. I didn't want him to catch a glimpse of me between the trees, shadowing him like a ghost. And oddly enough, he didn't. He had no idea I was there.

He walked through his last day on earth with equal pleasure and enthusiasm. He had built up an appetite by the time he saw the lights of the house glowing on his return, looked forward to the prospect of a good supper with Fanny. His appetite was never huge, but he'd promised himself a glass of port wine this evening as a well-earned treat.

He and Fanny sat at the table, discussing their latest plans for the house *Vailima*, and how they might spend Robert's birthday this year with the villagers. Should they throw a party?

Fanny lit another lantern and neither of them saw me slip into the room from the veranda. I was concealed by a thick curtain of shadow. Moths fluttered in the darkness, and there were haunting bird cries from the forest, but Fanny Osbourne and Robert were used to these noises by now.

Robert stood, and reached behind him for the bottle of port which sat waiting on the sideboard, but he stopped.

'What was that?' he asked Fanny.

He felt something, heard something pop inside his head.

He turned towards his wife and said, 'Does my face look strange to you?' but even as he spoke his features were slipping to one side and his words came out slurred, and Fanny watched in horror as I stepped out of the shadows onto the stage of life, and caught Robert in my arms before he fell. By the time I lowered him gently onto the boards he had stopped breathing. His spirit was gone. After all those years of dogging his footsteps, I took him by surprise, after all.

Fanny sank beside her husband and cradled his head in her arms. I stepped back, allowed her that much. They formed a strange tableau in the shadows of that wooden house on stilts, while the noises of the forest grew louder, and Fanny realised that her greatest adventure yet was now over.

Even then, Robert was reluctant to leave. He looked back at his wife, at the life he had made for himself on that verdant island in the South Pacific. He was king of all he surveyed: *Tusitala*, Teller of Tales. He did not want to leave it all behind. He wanted to take it with him. He loved life. I had a hard job of it persuading him to leave.

He had fought against me for months at a time, as he lay confined in his bed as a child, and then later as an adult, plagued by ill health. He wanted to be well, to live life to the full, and when he couldn't do that, he wrote down his adventures instead. In the pages of his books he sailed the high seas, eluded villains, and went in search of his own stolen heritage, defying the odds, seeking justice, triumphing over his enemies.

He followed me, at last, when he realised he had no choice, and left Fanny lying there, sobbing with her arms around the long lifeless body on the floor.

Yes, sometimes my work is heart-breaking, to be sure.

A Woolfish Tale

I am thinking now about a garden path in Sussex, which winds down to the banks of the River Oise. A middle-aged woman stood on the stones and looked out at the slow-moving water which lapped the shore. I was standing a few feet behind her, watching, but I desperately hoped I could prevent what was to follow.

However, it is not in my remit to interfere.

A plane flew low overhead, thunderous engines roaring, and as she watched it, she thought of how bombs fell. Her brother had died in Flanders in the first war, and now here she was, watching another war unfold, one which rained bombs onto her own beloved city. She and Leonard had moved out of London by now. But the war followed them.

The woman hesitated, and for one blessed moment I wondered if she might change her mind. I edged forward and round to look at her face. She had particularly sad eyes, hollowed out by a look of complete desolation – imposed on her by depressive illness. I could tell that much at a glance.

I think she knew I was there, but couldn't be bothered to look at me. I didn't blame her. She had no interest in me at all, but was simply taking her life into her own hands. She knew what she had to do.

I watched as she bent down and began to gather stones from the shore. At first, I hoped she would skim them on the water's surface, a playful game, but I should have known better. It was a vain hope. She picked up the heaviest, and filled her capacious pockets with them. Then she took off her hat and left it beside her cane, and began to walk forward, stumbling a little.

I watched her from the bank. The water was cold and it lapped around her ankles, seeped through her leather boots, soaked the skirts of her heavy coat, and the dress underneath it. But she didn't stop. She pushed forward again, into the river's slow embrace until it was up to her chest.

Now, I don't much like getting wet, but I waded in after her. It was my duty, after all. The water parted for me and I moved through it to stand beside her. She stopped, and I saw her blink several times, but again, she refused to look at me.

'Virginia.' I spoke her name very gently, but she didn't respond.

She had been obsessed with me for months now. I was all she could write about, think about, as the first German bombers flew low over the Sussex countryside. But it wasn't the onset of another war which drove her to take matters into her own hands. The voices had returned, and they made her feel sick and exhausted, unable to work. She couldn't bear not being free to read and write. She couldn't bear the thought of inflicting another episode on her loved ones. She'd had enough. She wanted peace.

So I stood beside her, chest-high in the water, and let her know I was there.

Still she would not look at me.

She stepped forward once more, and I felt the mud

beneath her feet give way, gently collapse and subside. The current swept around her, and took her. I saw her face underneath the water, through the brackish swirl. She and I and the river became one.

I bore her along in my arms and tried to offer a last consoling word, but Virginia was oblivious. She was beyond comfort, beyond peace. All she wanted was oblivion. Never before have I encountered a case so set upon their own destruction. Life had nothing left to give Virginia, and she had nothing left to give back to it, she believed. She wanted release, freedom from the chains of her own mental suffering.

So I broke those chains, one by one.

She was like a fish, a wolf in the water, a wolfish bird with gills and no feathers. I watched her transform.

Then she and I rose into the air, and Virginia watched, astounded, as her own body sank to the river bottom, and was dragged along by the strength of the current. The river took her, and washed her towards the sea.

Once Virginia was safely dispatched, I sat on the bank shivering. I almost caught a chill myself that day. Occupational hazards.

I like to hang around sometimes, observe the fallout. It seems respectful to those who are left behind.

Her husband found the hat and cane lying on the shore, several hours later. He had read her note by then, and understood.

Of Virginia herself, there was no sign.

I took the liberty of drifting into her study, examining her desk, her scattered snowstorm of papers. She'd just finished writing a novel. I inspected the title page. *The Waves.*

I read the last lines out of curiosity.

There was no one there to disturb me, as the dust motes moved in the sunlight. Besides, Leonard was a practical man, not the kind to notice *Yours Truly* lurking in the shadows.

'*Against you I fling myself, unvanquished and unyielding, O Death! The waves broke on the shore.*'

'Interesting,' I thought.

I understood what she meant. She was refusing to give in to her illness. She would not let it win. Instead, she would choose what would happen next.

The ocean almost claimed Virginia's body, but not quite. She nearly made it out to sea, into the vast green depths, and I almost wished she had. Instead, she was caught by some reeds, and banked against a distant shoreline, face down, like a black log, seaweed hair drifting, several miles from her home at Monk's House.

Some children were playing by the shore when they noticed her. One of them leant forward and prodded the corpse with a stick.

'Look,' he cried, 'A black coat.'

He pulled on it, turned her over, and that was when those three young lives were changed forever, lost their innocence, scarred by an experience that would never leave them.

I won't go into details, except to say that the river – while being a graceful goddess of beauty in herself – does nasty things to a corpse. Fish had eaten Virginia's face. She was bloated, swollen.

While I, of course, find the physical manifestations of decay a vaguely interesting and fascinating phenomenon, I know of course that you people do not feel quite the same way.

And nor did these three children.

There were screams, followed by shocked silences, and recurring nightmares which chased them into their adult years.

They got over it, of course. Children often do.

But it marked an end for them, and the beginning of a relationship with *Yours Truly*. They began to notice me in the shadows, became aware of my constant vigilance on the edges of the busiest and brightest arenas of public life. Always, I was there with them. I had left my mark, my calling card, and they knew I would be back one day to claim what is rightfully mine.

That's the way it works, I'm afraid.

Once you meet me, you never forget me.

Poets Old and New

After serving up this little delicacy for her readers, Marcia is keen for me to talk about other poets. Of course, Sylvia Plath leaps into her mind, but I don't really like to talk about that, the children in the other room, with their bread and milk on the bedside table, the door of the room sealed shut with tape to protect them, the window flung open to let in the fresh air. Sylvia's body lying prone on the linoleum, breathing in the noxious fumes from the oven. The naked light bulb hanging from a bare socket wire, swinging slightly, casting a lurid 1960s glow on the drab interior of her London flat. A death which could so easily have been avoided nowadays, with the silver strip of little white pills. Magical. Pop one in your mouth and you're cured. Addicted, but cured.

Such a waste. They didn't understand postnatal depression back then.

It happens to a lot of women.

How often I was there with her towards the end, whether she was sitting astern a small rowing boat on the waves of the ocean, walking the woodland paths near their rented farmhouse in Devon, or in the grim sepia-tinted streets of Sixties London. She bore her children, and she loved them, and she struggled to survive, to exist. And she wrote like a dream, but no one recognized it until after her death, of course, as is so often the way. Too busy admiring her husband.

There are other poets, of course, but they don't really have the subtle nuances of Sylvia's struggle.

T. S. Eliot, Marcia suggests?

I almost yawn out loud and mouth the word BORING! White middle-class privileged male – of course he became a respected poet. Where were the obstacles?

I am thinking now of the tender and subtle dignity of Leonard Cohen, who faced me head on like a collision, even though he did not want to die. I haunted him all his life, even in the freshness of his youth. Although he claimed that he was ready to die, he had to later retract the claim and admit he may have been exaggerating. Three weeks later I took him in the night, in the quiet of his home. I was there waiting for him in the corridor, as he rose from his bed in the night. Needed a pee. He didn't see me in the dark, just a lumpish shadow which gradually detached itself from the wall and there – suddenly – I was.

He knew me at once.

'I always knew you were a woman,' he said softly. 'They all think you're a man. Androgynous, sexless at best. But I knew it.'

He'd been singing my praises for years now, in beautiful lyrics and asides, beckoning me forward, daring me to step from behind the curtain and take centre-stage next to him, instead of hidden in the wings.

And now my moment had arrived and there was no spotlight on us. Just he and I in a warm dark embrace in the darkest hour of the night, when there was no one about to observe or complain or lament. And I took him.

He fell to the floor, and I was there in his arms, and he in mine, and no one saw us until the morning, by which time both he and I had fled and only a limp husk remained, all its memories and thoughts and feelings and long-lived tales melting away into nothing.

His voice is captured in song and poetry, in limitless recordings, TV footage, radio airtime, imprinted on CD and disc, etched onto glossy black vinyl, released on the air waves, and into the ether. His voice is still there, travelling through time, distinctively mournful.

But Leonard himself is gone. I took him. It was me.

I walked away with him in my arms, and left his family and friends bereft.

I couldn't help it. It was my duty.

I am at pains to explain all this, but there is a kind of beauty in it, as Leonard himself was so exquisitely aware.

The Young at Heart

I have lulled Marcia into a false sense of security. She is floating on the slipstream of the peaceful vision I've conjured.

I glance down at the flat screen, silently recording, and think of her readers.

I could tell them about the Vietnam War, but what is there to say? I could talk about boats full of refugees – those who fall between the cracks of nations, unwanted, dispossessed. I could talk about those in Uganda, executed for being born into the wrong body. I could talk about slave ships, packed to the gills with people in chains, poured into the hold as goods to be bought and sold. I could list the countries where tragedy strikes, and has struck over recent millennia.

Oh yes, you human beings think I am bad news, but you bring a whole new meaning to the concept. You don't need religious imagery of demons and devils to intimidate people. You created hell on earth all by yourselves. And you go on creating it, but will Marcia's readers want to hear about that, as they flick through the glossy pages of her magazine between coffee and brunch, sitting on the decking with hair still damp from the shower?

I let out a sigh, and she glances at me quizzically.

'I do appreciate it must be hard,' she says then. 'I'd never given it much thought before, but now that I've met you...'

I smile and nod, keen to reassure. I like to put people at their ease. I'm good at it.

'I've really enjoyed my stay in the hotel, by the way. It's not often I get to treat myself.'

'So glad you've got something out of it. You know, when I first responded to your offer I was a bit apprehensive,' she confesses. 'I'll admit that. It seemed such a bizarre idea.'

'Yes, I can see that,' I agree. 'I was just keen to put my side of the story. D'you understand?'

'Of course. It's an honour to be the one to...' She waves her hand, at a loss for words, and adds vaguely, 'you know.'

I smile at her for a little longer than necessary, but it doesn't appear to unnerve her.

'I hope you don't mind me asking but, do you have any children?' I risk asking her.

She shakes her head. 'I'm married to my job. You don't think I got to the top of this tree without some sacrifices, do you?'

'That's a shame,' I add.

She gives me a quick panicky glance.

'Why so?'

'Oh! No reason!' but I feel a surge of pity, that uncomfortable compassion again, which I make a point of hiding from her. No point in letting her know.

And now, suddenly, I want to tell her about Una, the cheerful, spirited young girl in Ireland, who was so full of life and fun.

She lived in Belfast, I tell Marcia. She had red hair and blue eyes and freckles, and her parents loved her. She was sixteen when she got pregnant by a boy she'd been seeing for a while. She went to her GP as soon as she found out, but he refused to help her. By law he couldn't, you see.

I came across her one day, weeping on a swing in the local play park, and I knew then she would suffer. Unable to get a legal abortion, she was too afraid to tell her parents. They were so proud of her for getting an unconditional place to study English at Dublin, so how could she break the news to them and destroy that dream? I listened to the creak of the chains as she sat on that swing under the hot August sun, and she didn't see me there, of course. As far as she knew it, she was alone.

She found the address: a block of flats with clothes horses full of wet washing on the balconies, dogs barking. She climbed the stairs and knocked on the door of a third-floor flat. It was opened by a middle-aged woman, a midwife by training: I didn't catch her name. Smells of cooking leaking into the hallway.

Una was made comfortable on a sofa bed, with plenty of pillows and a towel, while the abortionist got to work.

I didn't look. I'm squeamish about that sort of thing.

Una was quietly docile, biting her lip. She kept her mind focused on the future.

Afterwards, she took herself off home, lay down in bed, her womb empty, and slowly bled to death. She had all her life in front of her. Robbed.

Marcia grows pale.

'I suppose it was difficult in those days,' she murmurs uncomfortably.

I raise my eyebrows.

'It was last week,' I tell her. 'Una died last week. In Ireland.'

Once Marcia has recovered from her shock, I share with her another story.

'The young are always the hardest to take.'

And even as I speak, I find myself in that Beechcraft H18 airplane as it rumbles low over Lake Monona, on its way to Madison airport.

1967: a foggy December night. They were tired but happy, after several days of playing concerts at a club called Leo's Casino. Otis Redding was twenty-six, and had just finished recording his song *Sittin' on the Dock of the Bay*...

It had yet to be released, but he was already becoming famous as a music producer with Stax records, writing songs, performing, cutting vinyl. Not bad for a boy from the deep South who left school at fifteen to wash cars. Someone heard him singing in the car park once, while he was wiping down a hatchback, and was immediately convinced by his talent. A few years later and he was just about to hit the big time. He had a couple of television appearances booked for the following year, on *The Ed Sullivan Show* and *The Smothers Brothers Comedy Hour*. He was about to become a household name.

He wasn't particularly nervous of flying. He bought the airplane so he and his band members could tour.

The runway was polished to a shine, slick with rain, but the plane took off anyway.

Unbeknown to them all, and to my own deepest regret, I occupied the only empty seat. The young are so full of promise and hope, and their own invincibility.

It was a short journey. The Beechcraft flew low through muffling cloud, while the pilot peered anxiously through the windscreen, looking for pointers. He radioed through to Madison, asking for permission to land, and then on through the night, beginning to lose altitude in preparation for a landing which by now he was wishing to be over.

Otis leaned forward and gazed out of the window to his right at the lake shrouded with fog beneath him. As I slipped into the seat beside him, he didn't feel a thing. I wanted to warn him, I wanted to hold his hand, but I suppose the moment for that was past. I should have stopped him from boarding that plane: ordered them to call a halt to takeoff.

'Why didn't you?' Marcia interrupts.

'I told you – it's not within my power. If I once start that, where will it all end?'

With him were five young band members of the Bar-Kays, all teenagers: guitarist, tenor saxophonist, organist, drummer, session musicians all of them, on the verge of a bright new future, all of them in love with life.

I find myself listening to the lyrics of that song in my head, staring out of the misted porthole window, knowing that beneath us lies a treacherously wide lake, hidden by fog.

They are due to play at Factory Nightclub near the University of Wisconsin. It is the swinging sixties, and Otis is one of the best things to emerge out of Memphis, along with Elvis, of course. And Martin Luther King, who will be shot the following year.

He doesn't think it can happen to him.

No one ever does.

And it is to my eternal regret that I cannot warn you, as I could not warn him, the Prince of Soul himself.

Those lyrics played on and on inside my head, as the airplane hit the surface of the lake. The impact was sudden, but time enough to register the end and cry out 'Oh no!' while the debris scattered for miles, and Otis himself, still fixed in his chair, slipped beneath the mist to a watery grave, where they found him a few days later, still buckled into his seat, cold as the water he landed in.

Sittin on the Dock of the Bay was released a few days later to wide and rapid acclaim.

Headlines screamed out the news **The Prince of Soul is Dead**.

I'm sittin' on the dock of the bay Watchin' the tide roll away...

And then the words sink beneath the waves...

Marcia wipes a tear from her eye, looking pleased with herself.

'My readers will love that one,' she purrs. 'Well done!'

She says it like it's a personal achievement of mine, a glowing accolade I should be proud of, robbing a young man – several young men – of their future.

'I didn't ask for this role,' I remind her. 'I had greatness thrust upon me.'

'I understand,' she consoles me, aiming for a sympathetic grimace.

I flinch.

I don't know what makes me say it, but I add, 'I'm a lot older than I look, you know.'

'You're only as old as you feel,' she quips.

'I *feel* ancient!'

'Never mind,' Marcia comforts, and she glances around at our opulent surroundings. 'You should make the most of the facilities while you can!'

I take her point.

'How long are you planning on staying in Edinburgh?' she asks now.

'It really depends.'

'Our London office is green with envy.'

'I find that hard to believe, somehow.'

She nods enthusiastically.

'Oh yes, it's true.'

'Do you get down there often?' I ask.

'As often as I can, although I must admit I like it best, here in Edinburgh. We have an office in the New Town, now.' She shrugs. 'What's not to like? I walk to work. No stuffy Tube journeys for me.'

I remember hearing somewhere that Marcia is the proud owner of a little mews cottage in Dean Village, just below Stockbridge. I can imagine her leisurely walk to work in the morning. Heaven knows where I glean these snippets of gossip!

I study her calmly while her gaze is drawn to a painting on the wall: a Hebridean beach, white sand lapped by azure blue with a sprinkle of wildflowers in the foreground. What exactly occupies the mind of the Chief Editor of *A Class Act Magazine*? What fills her hours and her days, other than this kind of thing? And what fills those glossy pages, other than a graphic and revealing write-up based on her interview with *Yours Truly*?

'Would you mind if I took another headshot?' she asks, smoothly scooping her iPhone from the table top.

'Of course not!'

Smiling for the camera. More pics.

Much good may it do us.

'Are you on Twitter? Instagram?' she asks.

I shake my head. 'I try to avoid social media.'

'Quite right. Why should you? Drives me insane.'

Then the iPhone is replaced and returned to recording mode.

'Your battery's doing well,' I comment, nodding at her sleek technology.

'I charged it before coming out,' she assures me.

'Ever the pro!'

I'm shocked at my own easy camaraderie, my effortless deception.

Risk

'Families are fascinating things, aren't they?'

I slip into the background of your narratives without you even noticing. Sidelined, but there all the same. Some of you court risk and danger, like a drug. It's all down to personality types, I suppose.

Take the Collins family and their friends, the Burgesses, for example.

I was with the family when they woke up that morning, although they did not know it. They were middle-class, adventurous types, sporting brightly-coloured anoraks and puffer jackets – all the gear for expensive adventure holidays. They believed in getting out into the fresh air, in search of the buzz factor.

Two families, staying at a rented villa off the shores of Loch Lomond. A gaggle of young children with them, ages ranging between two and eight years. They sought security in numbers in an effort to keep the kids occupied.

They were all doctors, met at medical school in a previous life, before the arrival of offspring and parenthood.

One of the women was a little nervier than the rest. I noticed her straight away. Nails bitten down to the quick. While the others seemed supremely confident in themselves, very sure of their own worth, she was less so. It was as if there was something unfinished around the edges about her. She seemed to melt into the background.

'Louisa,' the other woman cried. 'It will be an absolute hoot. And let's face it, you and I get a break! Where's the worry in that?'

The supper table was littered with abandoned bottles of prosecco, tall fluted glasses, the remains of a roast chicken and a bowl of salad, broad white china smeared with left-over sauces and small heaps of gnawed bones.

Lucy and Katie were whining.

'Please, Mummy,' the eldest pleaded. 'Can we?'

Louisa watched the others, and I could see the fear there. I could *smell* it. Louisa's husband, Simon – familiar with his wife's nervousness by now – was impatient at her reluctance.

His look said it all.

'Why spoil it for the kids?' his expression seemed to say. All without words, of course. Couples can communicate these hidden messages, secret accusations, and I never miss a trick. I see it all, if I happen to be present at the feast.

As the two couples went to bed that night, Simon sat on the end of the bed, pulling his socks off. He dropped them in a sad heap beside his boxers.

'Louisa, you've got to be able to let go, let the kids live a bit. Take a leaf out of Gillian's book. *She* doesn't worry.'

'But the kids…'

'… it's an adventure for them. Don't fill them with your fear. Relax. God's sake, just relax.'

Louisa *tried* to relax.

'I suppose they should be allowed to have adventures, like we did. Take risks.'

'Exactly! Besides, where's the risk with both fathers in charge? Where on earth is the risk in that?'

'It's not like I don't want them to explore, to reach out on their own. That's what we did, after all. Climb trees, and all that. But...'

'But what?'

'The loch...' She looked at him. 'It's so deep.'

I knew what she meant. Even as she spoke I sensed the pull and draw of that fathomless darkness beneath the still waters, hidden currents ready to drag you under, tree branches reaching like dangerous antlers in the murky depths.

'Geoff and I are experts,' Simon reassured her, as he had reassured her many times before. 'We know what we're doing. We've been kayaking before. Lucy loves it. You know that.'

'What if one of them plays up, or over-balances?'

'It won't happen,' he promised. 'The worst never does.'

'How can you say that? You're a doctor!'

'That's exactly why I can say it.'

I left them to their eternal debate. There was no point in lingering.

I trod the soft corridors of the rented villa that night, checking up on the sleeping children. Lucy and Katie – offspring of Louisa and Simon – plus the three young boys belonging to Gillian and Geoff.

Doctors, all of them. High-achieving, high-earners, used to success, adventure, not afraid of risk.

If there was a loch beside their villa, they did not

want to skirt around the edges of it, throwing sticks for the dog, feeding the ducks, looking at the view along with all the feeble types. If there was a loch they wanted to be at the centre of it, to join the playground fun. They were shakers and movers, leaders, forerunners of society and they believed in raising their children to be the same.

They bought the best gear, indulged in the most expensive sports and no expense was ever spared.

They were brave, they were fearless, they were fun.

Only one of them was the spoiler of the party... poor Louisa who was always inclined to hold them back.

They all resented her just a little because she was the one who could not jump in, both feet first, without checking the water level. Simon often wondered how he had ended up with Louisa, for she hadn't always been afraid of life. Not like this. She had been fearless once, ready to embrace danger and risk. When he thought about it – if he bothered to think about it at all – he realised the change probably happened after their first child was born.

That's often when you become aware of *Yours Truly* floating on the periphery of your lives, a sudden glimpse of me which completely unnerves you, takes you by surprise.

I inspected the sleeping children in their beds, all tucked up, arms flung wide, mouths open, breathing softly, damp with sleep. A little tumble of bodies, like a litter of pups. It was hard to work out who belonged to who, genetically speaking, for they were all thrown together, a holiday of two families – always much more fun than one.

Security in numbers, as I said.

The next morning dawned bright and cloudless. A porcelain blue sky. Not a ripple of wind, not a drop of rain.

There was much laughter and hilarity as they assembled on the rocks below the villa, kayaks at the ready. Two long canoes that could carry four men apiece. The children were excited and ran about the shore, shouting and crying out to each other until Gillian told them to pipe down.

'And so, the adventure begins…' Simon smiled at Louisa, trying to ignore her fretful expression.

'Ah, the best sound in the world,' Gillian smiled, as they waved them off.

'What is?'

'Silence,' and she spun on her heel, and headed back up the rocks to the balcony of their villa.

Six steps up, and a welcome tray of tea and more prosecco awaited them. A pile of books, rugs folded over the backs of chairs.

Louisa stood on the shore, staring after the kayaks as they headed out into open water, one father at the helm of each, children on board with their brightly-coloured life-jackets on, their voices fading. Each child had a paddle, and even the little one was on board, which Louisa privately thought was madness, but if Gillian was prepared to allow that risk, then who was she to challenge her? A two-year-old, in a kayak? How would they manage?

But Geoff had been adamant he could cope.

He was the coping sort, had a strategy for every eventuality. He'd climbed mountains, scaled heights: parenthood was not going to hold him back.

I left the women to their break on the balcony and waited on the tiny tree-filled island in the centre of the loch, far away, where no one could see me.

Birds paddled nearby, the dip and sigh of water sucking against the rocks. So still, so peaceful. I almost enjoyed the lull, although of course I knew what was to follow. There was not a breath of wind on the surface. It stretched for mile after mile, pure and crystalline. Unusual, because quite often a keen breeze blows off its surface, but not today. Today was perfect for the two kayaking families.

Marcia is leaning forward in her chair.

'So, what happened?'

I shrug.

'The inevitable, of course.'

'Is it so inevitable?' Marcia asks. 'Don't families go kayaking all the time?'

'Yes, and many times they live to tell the tale. But in this case, unfortunately, not.'

'But there was no wind,' Marcia insists, and it occurs to me then how much more engaged she is by this story, perhaps because of the puffer jackets and the middle-class identity of the protagonists. Perhaps she can identify with their desire to conquer and rule the waves and teach their children to do the same.

I nod.

'There was no wind. No breeze at all, in fact.'

'So, how?'

'They started arguing. It only took one wobble and they were over.'

Geoff and the boys tipped and Simon watched in horror as their kayak remained floating upside down.

'Quick, Daddy!' Lucy screamed.

Simon made a grab for the other kayak with his paddle, then tried to remain calm.

'Look, you girls keep very still. I'm going to climb out and tip the other kayak upright again. Are you listening to Daddy?'

Both girls nodded, terrified, although Katie was sobbing uncontrollably.

Simon couldn't understand why Geoff had not been able to right the kayak, but of course he could not. He was underwater, diving down for his smallest son, the toddler, who had slipped effortlessly out of his life-jacket and down into the darkness.

I stood a long way off, on the little tree-covered island, watching, hoping, wishing they had listened to nervous Louisa's advice.

As Simon attempted to slide out of his own canoe in an effort to rescue the others, it too tipped, with the balance of probability, flipped like a coin, and in the panic that followed the two conquering fathers were simply unable to rescue all five children.

These Scottish lochs are deeper and darker than you imagine. They ebb and flow with hidden currents to drag you under, swirl you down into the subterranean depths, never to be seen again. According to Scottish myth, kelpies lurk here, dark mythic horses that will rise up from nowhere and pull you down when no one is looking. If you believe the legends… which I don't.

I am nothing if not rational. I know why these stories were told in the first place, to answer questions like this one. Where did those two families mysteriously vanish to? Why – with all their skill and confidence – did they not succeed in beating me at my own game?

Because life is a gamble, that's why.

You risk and you dare.

These two families were used to that sort of challenge; they were used to coming out the other side, unscathed. Just not this time.

The loch lay silent for miles around.

I waited until the last bubble broke the surface. Then all was still.

Across the water I heard a woman begin to scream. I don't know how she knew. I didn't bother to return to the villa, where the two women sat waiting on their balcony. I left them to it. My job here was done. But I imagine it ruined their holiday.

Marcia glances at me, deeply shocked.

'I thought you were the caring sort?'

'I am. But some people are just asking for trouble.'

She gazes at me, horrified, so I add, 'She did warn them. They should have listened.'

Faking it!

Marcia glances at her wrist-watch. That last anecdote has left her feeling uneasy. Perhaps my tone seems cruel. But what do you expect? I am Death Incarnate. I harvest the souls, I winnow and thresh. Young and old. Innocent and without guile.

'What's the biggest laugh you've ever had?' she asks now.

'Oh, that's easy. The biggest laugh I ever had was helping George Harrison to fake his own death. What a hoot that was.'

At last, a spark of envy in her eye. I put my head back and smile happily at the recollection. Summer days when the sun was still shining…

'But I thought…' she stumbles for words.

'He was dead? Yes – he is now. But he wasn't then, when his death made the news headlines. He went into hiding, quite understandably, of course. He was receiving death threats at the time. Most unfair. Memories of John, of course – what happened to him, in his prime.'

Marcia shakes her head sadly.

'I remember when John Lennon died,' she murmurs. 'I was doing my A-Levels at the time. Forty is too young – for a talent like that.'

I give a curt nod.

Let me paint you a picture, Marcia. There was I, along with Paul and Ringo, and George's wife, of course, and there was George. He'd been ill for a while. He was tired of it all, you know. He and his wife had been attacked in their own home – some stranger breaking in. He'd had to grapple with the man, took the knife off him. He was tired of the notoriety, of the fame. He remembered a time when he was just a boy – an ordinary boy – with only a guitar and no money, and no one knew him. And he wanted that freedom back again. There'd been death threats and he was worried for his wife and son, wanted the attention shifted elsewhere. He thought, if I'm out of the picture then maybe they'll leave us alone. Those were his exact words. I remember sitting in the front room of the mansion with them all, George's wife perched on the arm of the chair with her arm round him. They'd asked for my help. It was Ringo's idea, of course. These things always are.

'So what can I do to help, gentlemen?'

They glanced at each other.

Ringo shrugged.

'Make it look real. Make it convincing.'

'That won't be too difficult,' Paul added. 'He looks like death warmed up anyway.'

So, I wandered about the mansion, creating a certain ambience. Ringo started mucking about, of course. I turned a corner and there he was with a white sheet over his head, holes cut out for eyes.

I whipped it off him and said curtly, 'I think we're going to have to be a little more convincing than *that*.'

'What was it like, working with the Fab Four?' Marcia can't resist interrupting.

'Three!' I correct her. 'There were only three of

them by then. I had to become all school-marmish with them – keep them in line, you know. I was always telling them off, getting them to behave, but secretly I didn't mind. They were more mature by then, of course. They'd gone all sensible. Except Ringo, of course. He will never be able to do sensible, even when he's a very old man. And I hope to goodness he lives that long – because he's *such* a lovely man. So funny, and so unassuming. Laid-back, you know?'

'I can imagine,' she murmurs enviously.

So, on the night we faked it, we were all there in the hospital. George's wife dismissed the doctors, insisting on privacy in his last moments, that kind of thing. Her wishes were honoured, and we found ourselves gathered there in the clinical gloom of his private ward.

'Can't bear hospitals,' I confide. 'The smell of them gets to me. I don't know if it's the anaesthetic or what, but there's a certain chemical sting that hits the back of the nostrils. It gets to me every time.'

'Don't go all wobbly on us!' Ringo said, grabbing me by the elbow. 'We need you to man up a bit!' he added, and winked.

'Right, are you ready, Georgie boy?' Ringo asked our patient, who was lying back on his pillows looking suitably pale.

'I don't know, is it worth all the bother?' George said. 'If you leave me for long enough, I might just conk out anyway.'

I shook my head.

'You're not ready to join John just yet,' I told him. 'Believe me, I know.'

'Listen to the lady,' Paul said. 'She knows.'

I bridled slightly at Paul's patronizing tone, (I've never been comfortable with the term 'lady'), but I let it pass. I'm not one to cause a fuss. Live and let live, you know.

So anyway, George threw back the hospital sheet and revealed himself to be fully dressed with suitcases and passports at the ready, and I lay down in the vacant bed, still warm from where he lay. There was a lot of giggling and messing about.

'Come on, guys!' I muttered at them from the hospital bed. 'We need to focus.'

Ringo was fiddling with the saline drip.

'And will you leave that alone!'

I felt like their mother, all of a sudden.

It was then we heard a knock at the door, and we all froze.

Paul's eyes were so wide in his head I thought he was about to have a heart attack and that we'd have him to contend with as well.

'Er... just a minute,' George's wife called.

Ringo grabbed George and pushed him under the bed, where he lay ram-rod still, while Paul quickly manoeuvred the bedside cabinet to block the view.

I lay like a corpse, thinking myself into the body of a corpse-like George on the verge of extinction.

Then the door squeaked open and the doctor popped his head in.

George's wife sat on the bed, and held my hand.

'If you could just give us a few more moments, doctor,' she said quietly.

I felt the doctor's gaze sweep the room, glancing suspiciously at the suitcases.

Then Ringo began to sniff, which eventually turned into a sort of muffled weeping, to distract everyone. Paul began to pat him affectionately.

Don't overdo it, I was silently begging them. Too much grief would look obvious. But luckily, they were too famous to be questioned. Almost royalty, in fact.

Once the doctor left, the room sprang into action again. Ringo checked the coast was clear, dragged George from under the bed, helped him up, and away they scuttled, suitcase wheels rolling smoothly along the corridor. I heard the ping of the lift, and then they were gone.

I lay like a corpse until the doctors came, and George's wife informed them that she wanted to take the body home and did not require a funeral. It would be private, she declared. And her wish was their command.

And that's how we did it.

They took the service elevator, I think, heavily disguised of course. Ringo, Paul and George, their last fling, their last little adventure together, cheating the general public.

Oh Death, where is thy victory? Oh Death, where is thy sting?

After that, his wife dealt with the media circus, for a short while anyway, until the hullabaloo died down, and she was able to fly out to join him.

I went to visit them once.

They had a house on an island in the Canadian wilderness.

George's wife and son would join him in secret for holidays and birthdays, festive times of the year, you know, and the summer of course. He could have gone anywhere in the world, I suppose. His mansion remained empty. That's how he enjoyed the last few years of his life, far from the media glare, hidden in a forest, on an island, studying birds.

'Wasn't he bored?' Marcia asks. 'A man like that?'

'George? Not at all,' I tell her. 'Beautiful place to wait out the rest of your days. I've been there. Stunning.'

So, that's how I became involved in faking the death of George Harrison. Made a change, you see, to be cheating death, rather than harvesting another soul. Bit of light relief, to be honest. It doesn't matter if your readers find out the truth now. George is past caring. He got what he wanted. Five more years of anonymity before finally coming face to face with *Yours Truly* again. For real this time.

Of course, he knew me by then. He had befriended death and once you do that, it's not so bad after all, you see. So when I turned up that final time, he just smiled and said 'You again!'

'Yes, it's me, I'm afraid,' I replied.

It was the most peaceful death in the world.

I can see it now, blue skies, the shimmer of the lake, the movement of birds in the forest, and so much stillness... so much peace.

It's an enviable way to go, if you can arrange it.

Pause to Reflect

'Lovely,' Marcia murmurs. 'Just lovely.'

The tea cups sit between us, pushed aside, half-nibbled sandwiches left forgotten. She glances around for the waiter, who is nowhere to be seen.

'You must have had your busy periods,' she says now.

'Marcia, every day is busy in this business.'

'I know what you mean,' she smiles, although I really don't think she does.

'The Black Death, for example,' I tell her, and she visibly shudders. 'Sweeping across Europe, eliminating whole populations. We need a bit of a culling now and again, you see.'

My coldness shocks her, so I aim for an anecdotal approach. Share with Marcia and her readers the lightness of my passage through life, the lightness of my touch.

'Now and again,' I tell her, 'I come across a community of people who are such an example of bravery, it almost stops me in my tracks. Almost. But not quite. As I said before Marcia, I have a job to perform.'

'Of course.'

'And perform it I must.'

'Tell me what happened,' she says in her oily tones, almost like a counsellor trying to alleviate my pain.

So I transport her into the past, to a tiny seventeenth

century village in the Derbyshire dales, long before you had the benefit of satellites in the sky to communicate your news, or motorised vehicles to speed you on your way.

Quarantine

I came jolting along in a cart, wrapped in a bale of cloth on a warm wet day in August, following a summer of fever and failed crops.

I remember the journey well.

The carter didn't know I was there, of course. He'd transported the package all the way from London, as he was paid to do, and had no inkling of the deadly cargo he carried. He had no idea I was a passenger on board.

His was a humble existence. He leaned forward on his narrow perch and encouraged his horse to keep moving over the rough track to the address he'd been given in the Derbyshire dales.

I sat back and enjoyed the ride, admiring the view of the green sward as it opened towards the dales where the little village of Eyam nestled safely in its folds – a little like the fleas we carried in the folds of the bolt of cloth.

We rolled up outside the Hadfield house where the tailor lived with his wife. The parcel of cloth was delivered, and I stepped down silently from my place beside the carter and bid him a fond farewell.

He ignored me, of course.

He was completely unaware I had been his travelling companion throughout our rather pleasant but silent journey, stopping to sup at the same inns, sleeping in the same lodgings.

He hitched his horse, and carried on.

I, however, stepped down into the the Hadfield's cottage, along with the bolt of cloth.

'George,' Mrs Hadfield cried. 'Can you see to the cloth?'

George Vicars, the young tailor's apprentice, opened the parcel.

I stood aside and watched him, taking note of my surroundings. It was a small bare room, unadorned, not much in the way of furnishings, which was often the case back then. Chairs, a table, a dresser with some clay and earthenware cups and plates on it, jugs, a large black kettle beside the fire.

George lifted the cloth to his nose and inhaled. A terrible stench came off it where the rain had got through. The cloth was damp so he bent towards the fire, riddled the ashes and laid more wood. I watched as the flames began to build.

Mrs Hadfield looked in on him and said, 'My word, George. Do we need such a blaze?'

'Tis to dry out the cloth, Mrs Hadfield. It smells bad.'

He lifted it in the air and the stench unfurled towards his mistress.

She nodded and left him to his work.

He unrolled the cloth, wafted it outwards, and lay it before the fire on the backs of two chairs.

An odour of musty wool rose into the enclosed space, and immediately the fleas began to bite and George began to itch.

He itched and scratched and slapped the back of his

neck, and I watched him from where I stood beside the window.

The fleas were hungry, and they were nipping.

George was aware of them as an irritant. Fleas were not uncommon, just one of life's daily inconveniences, an everyday nuisance to be endured.

By evening the cloth had almost dried, though it was still a little damp in places.

'There,' George said, putting his nose to the cloth. 'Don't smell quite so bad now.'

I opened the outer door and took a stroll through the narrow country lanes, bordered by little cottages, which were soon to become so familiar to me.

Might as well settle in, I told myself, before the hard work begins. I'll be here for a while yet.

A scene of rural contentment unfolded before my eyes. I saw a young maid leading a cow, another scattering grain for a few scratching chickens, and chiding a goat with the personality of a stroppy teenager.

I saw fields fairly bristling with yellow haystacks and a barrel full of apples leaning against a barn wall, just gathered from the orchard, ready to make cider or pies. They were browning in the air and looked set to be sour rather than sweet, but these things do not concern me.

I don't have the privilege of a ravenous appetite.

I watch you mere mortals tuck in to your flitches of bacon and your loaves of sweet bread, and I envy the pleasure you feel, the delight, the anticipation.

As I have said before, I am merely a bystander. I do not salivate or feel the juices rising. My mouth does not water, my stomach does not growl, my throat feels no thirst.

When you crumble white cheese between your fingers, or sip clear ale from a pewter jug, I watch in fascination, feeling nothing but a calm sense of observation: fact-recording, note-taking, assessing.

There were children standing in the lane in the evening sunlight, playing where the doors of the cottages stood open.

Glancing in at one, I saw a family of eight gathered near a table not large enough to accommodate them all. The younger children played on the floor, eating what was handed down to them, the woman sat aside in an easy chair, making room for her husband and mother-in-law. They shared a pot between them, and each dipped a fork or a spoon, helping one another to eat. A scene of squalid contentment.

They were used to overcrowding. They slept at night in a tangle of bodies, some beside the fire, others in the box-bed behind a curtain. Brothers and sisters could only sleep when they felt the sigh of their siblings' breath in their faces. Their bodies warmed each other, like pups in a litter.

There was no privacy. How they managed to bear so many children is beyond me, a quick unobserved fumble in the darkness, when the only illumination came from the dying hearth. Muffled movements. Not too much shuffling. No grunts or moans, although the children were used to the antics of the farmyard animals and knew about the beasts of the field, how they copulated with brief grunts, and gave birth with a deep sighing moan as their offspring dropped into the straw. So if the family guessed at the noises in the night, they made no comment and thought nothing of it. It was life.

It was how they lived their lives, close to nature, part of it, wrestling a living from its soil.

As I observed the family in the calm honeyed glow of the early evening, their lives seemed untouched yet by grief. They knew want and hunger and hard work and worry, but in a few weeks' time Mrs Riley would look back upon this evening as a time of rare paradise, like Adam and Eve before the Fall. This – did she but know it – was bliss, to have all of her family around her, her children aged between seventeen and three years old, living and breathing.

In a few months' time – by April of next year – she will bury them all herself on a plot of land not far from this cottage, which will become known as the Riley graves. She will dig the seven graves herself, as instructed by the curate, and all seven of them, including her husband, will be laid in the deep earth by her own hand, and the soil shovelled back over their bodies, all within the course of a seven day period. One after the other they will fall, and one after the other Mrs Riley will bury them. Then she will leave this village and her house behind, never to return again.

I, sadly, do not know what it is to lose so much, to grieve so bitterly, as I've never had to give of my heart before. To love is to risk, as you humans are fully aware; unfortunately, that risk has never been asked of me.

All I do is watch. I never take part. I'm never centre stage.

('Does that hurt?' Marcia asks suddenly.

'Yes, it does a bit,' I admit. 'It really does.')

In April I will stand on the green sward beside Mrs Riley and watch her shovel earth onto the bodies of her children, and I will be there with her, whether she knows it or not.

Death-in-Life.

It is all one to me.

And to you, in the end. You can do nothing to change any of it.

And neither, sadly, can I.

That evening, after a peaceful stroll in the waning sunlight, I returned to the home of the tailor.

It was late August, and the harvest had yet to be brought in. It was a time of plenty and abundance.

There was laughter in the air. Children played, chickens scratched in the earth and chattered to one another. Wood pigeons burbled in the treetops. In those days of course, your forests and lanes were teeming with wildlife, full of birdsong, trilling, burbling, rising and falling. Even the corncrake added its musical note to the orchestra, and was such a common and familiar sound that nobody then remarked upon it.

Nowadays, of course, bird-twitchers with binoculars trample wheatfields and stake out beside meadows in the Hebrides in order to hear their cry – like a nail being dragged through the teeth of a steel comb, I'm told – or even more rare, to catch a glimpse of the bird itself, which is in fact a very dull creature, not remarkable at all.

The village of Eyam went about its business that evening, and those who glimpsed me passing the open door of their cottage, wondered briefly who the visitor might be, but when they observed me turning in at the door of the tailor's cottage, assumed I must be a traveller come to do business, a yarn merchant perhaps.

For my sex is not always apparent, as I have said, and my androgynous appearance can deceive.

Many of you catch a brief glimpse, and then I am gone, before you have had time to assess my age, sex, defining characteristics.

I came in at the door of the Hadfields, and there he was, young George Vicars the apprentice, measuring out and cutting cloth.

Only a faint stale aroma hung about the cloth now, sweetened by sprinkling a little rosewater onto it. Mrs Hadfield applied a hot iron to smooth out the creases, making the material easier to work.

The fleas had stopped biting; the dry husks of their little bodies had fallen into the cracks between the flags after their brief existence on this earth, to be swept up later. They had served their purpose. They had carried the disease from faraway London, and had left their calling card within the bloodstream of George Vicars, as he quietly worked away.

Dust motes danced in the open doorway, and the last of the evening sunlight slanted onto the flags.

Mrs Hadfield placed a jug of cider at his elbow.

There was another hour left of good working light, before it would be too dim to sew. He was making a new coat for the rector and already had the measurements to hand.

Dusk fell, the lantern was lit, and darkness fell across the fields.

Next morning George felt a little strange in his mood, his head thick with fog. He wiped his brow and thought nothing of it.

'It's close today,' Mrs Hadfield observed.

And that explained it.

The heat of late summer.

'Perhaps we shall have a hard winter of it, then,' Mr Hadfield added. 'Snow and blizzards.'

'And how do you work that one out?' Mrs Hadfield asked her husband.

'The berries!' He nodded his head towards the lane beyond their cottage.

'I took a walk yesterday and observed the mistletoe already had thousands of red berries upon it. And the rowan tree, too. God's way of providing for the birds. Nature's larder!'

'Perhaps,' his wife replied. 'But I wonder that you can find time for a stroll in the woods when the new bolt of cloth has arrived, ready to be worked.'

'George has it in hand, have you not? He is learning the trade.'

George said nothing. His head had begun to ache.

Two days later, when George did not rise from his truckle bed in the corner of the room, Mrs Hadfield inspected his sweating brow, noticed the purple contusions under his armpits and at his throat, and she paled.

'William,' she cried. 'We need the doctor.'

They both stared down at the young apprentice.

'It is too late for the doctor,' Mr Hadfield murmured sadly. 'We need the rector.'

Twenty-four hours later, George was dead, the first to fall victim to the plague in the quiet little village in the Derbyshire dales, where a deadly bolt of cloth had arrived only days before.

And so I picked my way down the country lanes from cottage to cottage, visiting them in their beds where they lay, picking off eight one week, seven the next, until the mounds of the dead rose higher.

The curate met with the last incumbent of the parish and together they drew up a plan of action.

They met in the church, and I slid in beside them on the bare wooden pew, interested to hear what they had to say.

'It is God's visitation upon us, William,' the old incumbent said.

'Well, whatever it is, there are measures we must take,' said the new rector. 'We have a duty to prevent the contagion from spreading to other villages.'

William Mompesson, the new curate, had taken over from Thomas Stanley a couple of years earlier. What he did not know was that his young wife would lie beneath the sod too, before winter was over. She would die battling the disease which ravaged her husband's parishioners, helping to nurse the sick until her own time came.

I watched the amber sunlight spearing through the high glass window onto the bare flagged floor of the church – everywhere was oak and timber and stone and dust motes – and felt a sigh of relief.

I prefer it when you endeavour to take matters into

your own hands, when you attempt to stop me in my tracks.

So they drew up three conditions.

There must be no more burials in the churchyard: from now on, families must bury their dead on their own land or in their own garden.

There must be no gatherings of people: the Sunday service must take place out in the open air, at Cucklet Delf, instead of the enclosed space of the church building.

And lastly, no one must be allowed to enter or leave the village.

'We will need to obtain the villagers' consent for this,' the curate said.

'It will be a hard thing to ask of them,' Stanley observed. 'To stay here – and die,' he added quietly.

A meeting was called. I heard the bell tolling, which would gather them on the green. Many looked frightened, their terrified faces stoical beneath their shawls and caps.

They agreed to the quarantine and went quietly back to their homes to await their fate. Again, I marvelled at your human resilience.

The lanes of the village became habitually deserted. No one went abroad or from house to house to find out who was ailing or well. Each household kept to itself.

The Rileys thought they had been spared because their cottage was a little distance from the rest, in a field all on its own. This gave Mrs Riley reason to hope as winter wore on.

Fragments of snow drifted on the air. Mr Hadfield had been right about the winter, although he was no longer here to see it. The bright berries were stripped by the birds and the snow fell, and sickness visited each house in turn.

They read their Bibles if they could read, muttered about the Angel of Death passing over, and had no idea I looked in at the window and watched them reading by the light of a single candle, the heavy book lying open on the table between them, too heavy to hold, as the father read to his family, and the children listened.

I am no Angel. I do not boast wings, although my journey through time is swift.

I blinked my eyes and watched and wondered – just like them – who would be next.

I suppose I am a little like Peter Pan. I have no shadow, no sex, although I identify more as female than male; I am timeless, but fixed in time. I do not age or grow weary.

I fly in at the window when you least expect, and fly out again, taking your children with me.

But I mean no harm.

I bear no ill will.

I do not mean to be sinister.

I simply do what must be done.

The villagers observed the strict quarantine. Outlying communities left food or goods at the boundary stones, but they never saw a soul. Coins would be left in the hollow of a rock filled with vinegar. There were no transactions or communication from those inside the village, with those outside. No one knew what was really going on in the village of Eyam: who lived, who died, who perished, who was spared.

I used to follow a young woman called Emmott, as she was of particular interest to me.

She appeared to have survived the bleak winter months surprisingly well so far, but she was sad at heart. She had a sweetheart in nearby Stony Middleton whom she longed to see, but the pair were not allowed to meet. Emmott pined.

But Emmott also had a secret.

I had had occasion to observe her before now, slipping out from the village at odd times, and wandering up to the green sward of the Delf, high above the houses. She would look back at the clustered rooftops tucked beneath, and sit on the grass, and wait.

Something was afoot here, I was certain.

Sure enough, a thin whistle penetrated the air, and Emmott sat up, alert.

Her face was pale with fright, and she glanced over her shoulder fearfully, but no one had followed her – so she thought, except *Yours Truly*, of course.

She knew Death stalked the village, picking off its residents one by one, arriving willy-nilly at a particular household before moving on to the next, but she was not one of those who had seen the dark visitor passing by an open doorway, or glancing in at a low window. She was fortunate in not being gifted with such visionary insight.

She felt guilty, I could see at a glance. She shouldn't be here.

She did not dare speak, or cry out, but she glanced across the rocks and saw him standing there. I pursed my lips and tutted, but who was I to judge?

He was here: Rowland Torre, her young sweetheart from the neighbouring village.

They stood in silence regarding each other across the space which divided them.

Such a look of longing in their eyes, on their faces, and they spoke not one word. They knew this much, to keep a good distance, and though they were breaking the rules, they knew where to draw the line. They could look, not touch. They dare not even speak, but stood gazing at a distance of several yards, with the rocks as a barrier between.

Rowland did not speak. He just gazed at the girl he loved, and she gazed back.

They did not draw any closer, and they made no noise for fear of discovery.

And I watched them from Emmott's side of the rocky barrier.

So this was where she had been vanishing to, slipping away between the trees, up into the hills, to Cucklet Delf above the village.

Every day they met like this.

'When this quarantine is over,' he called across to her once, 'then we will marry in the spring, and this terrible winter will be forever behind us.'

'We will tell our children about it,' Emmott replied, 'and our grandchildren,' and she imagined a warm hearth and a swept floor and a dresser full of winking pewter dishes and a chest full of linen, and her sweetheart beside her at night in the warm nest of the box-bed, with no barrier of rocks between.

Never again would they be parted, even for a single night, and this dreadful ordeal would become part of their family folklore, told to future generations as the seasons changed and the year turned full circle.

Do you remember the time? they would say.

I hoped, oh how I hoped that my assignment would not lead me anywhere near the door of the Sydoll's cottage that winter.

Snow fell, and still Emmott continued to beat a path from the village at the same time every day and Rowland would be there, waiting for her.

And so it continued well into the spring.

Surely, now, we will be spared, the remaining villagers thought. We have endured the cruellest winter of our lives. The pestilence will move on and leave us alone, unless of course it intends to make sure that not one of us is left standing.

The village of Eyam was eerily quiet. When traders brought food and left it at the boundary stone, they half-expected to see the last parcel of food still rotting there, disturbed by crows and hunting foxes, but instead it was gone, and there – as usual – would be the few coins soaking in vinegar, as payment.

But the village itself was so still. The dale in which it rested gave off no sounds at all of occupation or industry. No tapping of the blacksmith's tools, or barking of dogs; no clack of the homemade loom. Nothing. Not a voice. Not a child's cry.

Even the birds were silent.

And although it was so cold, no smoke drifted on the air.

One solitary thatched roof emitted a trail of smoke, where someone clearly still had the energy to light a fire. It formed a grey silk skein which unravelled above the village.

Stillness.

Silence.

It caught you by surprise.

It didn't seem right.

Meanwhile, I was kept very busy, going in at the door of one cottage, and out the next, laying a hand on each fevered brow.

The stench was awful, children and the elderly lying in their own filth, unable to tend to themselves, and no one to comfort them or bring a sip of water.

I came in at one door and paused.

The usual desolate scene confronted me, bodies lying where they had died.

Then I heard a croak and saw a faint movement. A young woman lying by the hearth lifted an arm and uttered one word.

'Water?'

She could see me as clear as day, and indeed why would she not?

I glanced frantically around the room, but the bucket was empty. Grabbing it, I went outside to the well.

By the time I came back, carrying the precious water in my arms, the young woman was dead. She had left, and I should have been there to see her on her way.

Her body lay on the floor, an empty husk, but she herself was standing on the threshold watching me, gazing at the room she had just quitted.

She turned out of the door of the cottage and walked away, and it was then I recognized her.

This was the little maiden who climbed in secret

to see her sweetheart every day on the hill above the village.

Up at the Delf, I saw the young man waiting by the rocks at the usual time.

When Emmott did not appear, he waited a while longer before sadly abandoning his post.

It was early spring and the buds were beginning to uncurl on the trees, but in the village of Eyam all was silent. No one celebrated the turn of the season, or looked forward to what the next few months might bring. For those who survived, it was winter in all of their hearts.

The quarantine was not over and would continue for a while yet.

The following day Rowland appeared again at the Delf, on his side of the rocks, and gave out his lonely whistle.

No one came.

I watched him and longed to be able to tell him, but what good would it do to crush his hope now? It would not end his pain.

The next day, and the next, he called across the rocks in hope that Emmott would call back. Perhaps she had sickened, but recovered? Or perhaps she had been helping to nurse the rest of her family struck down by the sickness? Once she was well again, or able to, she would appear beyond the rocks and answer his call.

But a week passed, and another, and still Emmott did not appear.

I stood and watched him.

I was interested to see how the human heart fares

under these woeful conditions. It can be useful in my line of work to have all of the facts before me, and be able to gauge how you react to loss.

After three months, Rowland gave up hoping. Now he arrived at the rocky knoll above the village simply to grieve, to mourn the loss of his love, for he knew by now she would not appear – not this day or the next, or the one after that.

As I watched Rowland grieving and hoping, it was then I noticed a thin figure standing far off among the trees. She was unchanged, as clean and bright as the day I first saw the young sweethearts. She gazed and she gazed at Rowland, but – sadly – he did not see her at all.

I caught my breath. How had this one managed to slip through? A rogue spirit drifting where it pleased, back to the place that really mattered, where her hopes and dreams had become crystallized.

She walked out from between the trees and went steadily forward to the spot where Rowland waited. She stepped over the rocks which had separated them in life, clambering with perfect ease, and hopped down onto the other side.

She stood facing him.

It was to my great sorrow that I realised Rowland neither saw nor sensed her presence. When she stood before him and placed her arms about his neck, he felt nothing, not even the cold kiss she planted on his lips.

Rowland came back to that spot every day for a year, but after that he stopped coming, and Emmott would stand there alone, waiting for him.

The living cannot grieve forever.

I have observed this.

Years later, when the ravages of the plague had moved on and Eyam was left in peace with its tragic history, an old man climbed up to the Delf and sat there on the rocks.

It was Spring. He had grown-up children now, and a wife.

But on this day he saw the spirit of a young girl in the first bloom of youth, and this time he recognized her.

By the time the plague left the little village of Eyam and the quarantine was lifted, it had claimed the lives of more than half the population. The Reverend William Mompesson's young wife was among the dead.

But the measures the two men took prevented the plague from spreading to surrounding villages.

In London, the deadly contagion thrived and multiplied and continued to run its course, clawing its way into the bloodstream of the living, transforming soft tissue into sponge and rotting matter for the worms to feed on.

It was a terrible year for all.

But I have never forgotten the year I spent in that Derbyshire village, watching the people of Eyam die. I walked among them silently, and when I left, they left too.

Cure

It was midnight in Pudding Lane. Thomas Farriner was tired after a long day producing his usual quota of bread for the neighbourhood and did not see me standing in the shadows as he prepared for bed. I stepped forward and surveyed the room.

The dark hollow of the oven was swept clean, ready for tomorrow's baking to begin before dawn, a few coals still glowing in its depths.

'See that the stove is doused,' he murmured to the servant, Esther, and made his way wearily up the creaking staircase to his room above.

Esther sat dozing beside the warmth of the fire with the cat in her lap. She was asleep when I stepped forward and blew onto the little flame.

A tiny red spark lifted into the air.

I watched as it landed on the basket of logs nearby, where it smouldered nicely.

But why, I hear you cry?

You see, in the random chaos of events I sometimes have a plan.

How else was I supposed to stop the plague from spreading? One hundred thousand inhabitants had already fallen prey to its ugly maw, the purple buboes swelling at their throats and groins and in the cavity of their armpits, sore and suppurating. Some miracle was needed to halt the deadly outbreak in its path. And that miracle was – *Yours Truly.*

The log basket began to crackle. Suddenly, in a burst of childish glee, I found myself prancing around the flames, fanning them into a little blaze so that sizzling tongues of it reached out and lapped at whatever wooden furniture it could find. It crawled up the wooden walls like an orange snake – several orange snakes – curling and twisting like a living thing.

It was alive – and so was I – capering in delight with my arms flung wide in a wild dance of abandon.

It was exhilarating to really let myself go like this, to throw caution to the wind and take leave of my senses.

Nothing else mattered but to see this flea-ridden, rat-infested city burn with all its rotting corpses inside.

By the time Esther woke and alerted the rest of the household, it was too late. Thomas Farriner beat at the flames and threw buckets of water from the barrel, but of course, the rush of oxygen served only to fan the blaze.

It was too late to save the bakery. The narrow wooden building burned and from its windows licked tongues of flame, reaching across to its neighbours in a hot embrace.

Thomas Farriner and Esther ran screaming into the yard, and others gathered in the street, ready to do battle with the flames.

The rest of London slept on, unaware of the danger they were in.

By the time the fire had spread outwards to a single square mile of Pudding Lane, the noise and the choking soot had gained in power.

A sheet of sizzling red billowed in the sky; curtains of vermillion and gold rippled, casting a glow of radiance on all that moved. And the noise. It roared and surged like the sea, a monstrous dragon.

Rats burned.

I saw their little charred bodies lying in the dingy alleyways, touched one with my toe in passing, turned over its little corpse.

The fleas on its back had burned too, into crispy flakes of nothingness. Defeated. Destroyed.

But as fleas are rumoured to have no souls, I was not especially engaged by this. Invisible to the naked eye, they dissolved into a light dusting of powder that became one with the ash and drifted on the smoke-filled air, vanishing into the night.

While their city burned, the rich slept on.

The Mayor of the town was not overly concerned when he was woken by an anxious provost bringing him the bad tidings. In a world which relied on lamps for its illumination, fires were common, started by a candle tipped against a bed curtain, a spark from a neglected hearth, a spillage of oil from a lantern.

'Another fire?' the Mayor muttered, still half-asleep. 'A woman will piss it out!'

Then he rolled over and went back to sleep, while the guzzling monster grew greedier still, devouring everything in its path. A Chinese dragon, writhing, curling, quivering in the heat it created.

It had been a long, hot, dry summer and on this September night the wooden houses, packed tightly together, were a tinder box waiting to be fired by the first spark.

Have you ever watched a fire burn?

Even in the hearth it has a life of its own, dancing

and shape-shifting, reaching up colourful fingers, deep blue and green within the red, popping and cracking, twisting and contorting.

Once unleashed from the confines of oven or stove it becomes a devouring monster, an all-consuming force of nature, which lives... until it dies. Windows which contained glass exploded outwards and flames crashed through, reaching across narrow streets to where buildings opposite almost met overhead.

The Thames itself was alight, and still the Mayor slept on.

No woman would piss this fire out.

This fire was started by *Yours Truly* and I did not intend to see it smoulder for nothing.

If lives were lost, that was the price we had to pay.

But it's not you who are paying the price, I hear you cry.

Oh, but it is.

That fire kept me busy for days on end, without pause or rest. I was absolutely exhausted afterwards.

It has been my lot in life to feel compassion for those I must take – my curse, if you like, and if I could thwart the progress of the Black Death, then I would, by whatever means it took.

The sky above London roared, so that night became brighter than day. There were distant cries of panic, screaming, shouting, as people fled from its approach.

Rumours began to circulate through the panicking crowds that terrorists were responsible, it was some kind of incendiary attack. Hadn't there been foreigners infiltrating the city in recent months: the Spanish, the French, the Dutch?

I watched, helpless, as hysteria gripped them and a young Spaniard was dragged from his house and lynched in front of a crowd of jeering onlookers.

What is it about you lot that you must always find someone to blame, preferably the foreigner, the stranger among you? Suspicion rules your heart, and in times of crisis you mete out your own form of rudimentary 'justice'. There was nothing I could do. You make your own tragedies.

When it became clear the raging fire was completely out of control, a stampede began: people dragged carts full of possessions, anything they could carry, down to the river to escape its path and save what they could. Boats were so overcrowded they sank or overturned; fights broke out.

Cartwheels rumbled over the cobbles, adding to the chaos.

Those who could see me pushed me aside.

One woman grabbed my arm and cried, 'Get out of the city. Don't you know it's in flames and we'll all die?' Her eyes were wild.

By the following morning she would be lying on the cobbles, half her body crushed beneath an overloaded cart unfortunately tipped over in the pandemonium.

I could see the scene of her demise as I looked into her eyes that night – a death foretold – but there were further screams, and in an instant she was gone, borne along by the crowd.

We would meet again when she least expected it, and then she would remember my face.

None of you are wheat or chaff, sheep or goats.

All those parables, the language and religious

imagery you employ to help you understand or make sense of your own mortality, none of it matters in the end.

You are all one and the same.

You all fall to my touch, my dark embrace.

None of you will be ready for me.

I am truly sorry it has to be like this.

But none of this was my idea.

'So fascinating,' Marcia breathes, and suddenly I am transported back to the present moment and the delicious comforts of our little corner of The Balmoral.

We are surrounded by marble and clean modern lines, carefully arranged flowers, dazzling mirrors. The screams and chaos of a burning city slowly fade and the contrast is exquisite. Long windows allow the correct level of diffused daylight through, surfaces are polished until they gleam; there is the hint of an aroma of lemon and thyme, slightly antiseptic but delicately sensual.

The deep pile of the carpet softens every sound and seems far removed from the blazing wooden city I remember.

'To actually be there, at these times of great danger...' she murmurs.

'Well, yes, that is my occupation.

'A bit like a journalist, I suppose. I interviewed Kate Adie once,' she muses. 'Incredible woman. The career she's had.'

I nod sagely.

'What was it like?' she adds.

'It was hot,' I answer truthfully. 'And very bright. The sky was lit up like the brightest day.'

'Awful,' Marcia sighs. 'Wonderful!'

I decide to confide in her, reveal a little more of my true self. The mark of a professional journalist, I suppose, is that she can encourage me to give more than I intend.

'The fire was beautiful,' I confess, 'despite the suffering. It ripped and tore. Such beautiful colours! The screams, the smoke inhalation, none of that is a pretty sight, I'll grant you, but the fire itself was a spectacle. London was lit up for that night and several nights afterwards. It took four days to bring it under control. They had to explode buildings in its path to halt its progress, but even this didn't work. Nothing could stop it. The King had to request the help of his brother and the army, but by then it was too late. You could see across from one side of the city to the other and within its walls only charred embers remained, smoking faintly in the eerie dawn.'

There is a pause while Marcia digests this.

'But one thing was certain.'

She looks at me, waiting for what I will say next.

'The Plague had gone... for a few years, at least.'

'Another scone?' she offers, leaning forward.

I politely decline. 'I'm stuffed. Couldn't manage another thing.'

I notice the young waiter in the distance, serving an elderly couple across the far side of the room. His manner is professionally deferential, masking an air of boredom. He won't be doing this job forever. He is saving up for his scooter and then he will be off, heading for the blue beyond, before beginning the next phase of his journey...

'There are so many stories I could tell you, Marcia. So many.'

'Well, I wish we had more time,' she purrs.

'Ah, time! We could all do with more of that…'

And with this, I decide to serve up another historical footnote.

The Schoolhouse

I think now of an isolated schoolhouse far from town or city, the winds howling past the corner gables.

A rush mat lies on the bare flags and a stove burns at one end. The school mistress has wood and kindling stored in readiness. The benches are empty, waiting for the few students to arrive from the neighbouring farms and crofts.

Miss Gent prepares her classroom, which is also her home. She sleeps in a corner, screened off by a curtain. She was lucky to get this position. It was either this, or being the governess to a family of rich industrialists in Dundee who treated her badly. The children called her rude names, and if she approached the Mistress to complain of their behaviour, Mamma took the part of her dear offspring and encouraged their bad habits.

Miss Gent wears a grey twill dress, buttoned up to the neck. Her hair is combed precisely with a straight middle parting and bound tightly behind. A woollen shawl keeps off the chill.

She listens to the wind howling and waits for the pupils to arrive, wondering who will attend this time and who will be kept at home to help with the chores or farm work.

She clatters the pile of slates onto the front desk. She has a map on the wall, also a globe of which she is inordinately fond, and some heavy leather books on a shelf.

She has not been teaching here long and feels a touch nervous, a flutter of butterflies inside her belly. She has to remind herself she has nothing to fear. They are merely children and this is her domain. She is mistress of all she surveys.

It is a lonely life, however.

The curate provides her with all she needs in terms of food and fuel. He visits occasionally to ensure the new school mistress is getting along nicely in her new position. The Reverend Mackay is very proud of himself in taking measures to ensure the local children have a school to attend and a teacher to educate them. Miss Gent seemed like an ideal candidate for the post. She speaks French, is well-educated; the daughter of a minister herself, she is the possessor of fine accomplishments. She draws, plays the piano (although there is none here at the schoolhouse – it would be impossible to transport one across the moors). She is keen to get her pupils to recite poetry, to express themselves through music and song, to learn botany and the sciences – but first of all she must teach them to read. And to copy out their letters, learn the alphabet, one by one.

She has innovative ideas. She has decided that if her pupils are allowed to decorate each letter in the manner of old illuminated manuscripts they might have seen in the chapel, then they will take more pleasure in their work. The pleasure felt in performing this task will embed it more firmly in their memories, she believes. So, when they learn the letter A, for example, they are allowed to decorate it, to draw it as if it is a person, or an object, coming to life – one which has relevance in their own lives. A crow, for example, for the letter W. Or a dragon for the letter S. Or a house with a chimney for the letter H. In this way, she believes, they will remember their letters more easily. However, she hasn't yet got as far as W. Progress is slow.

So it is simple tasks she sets them.

But the process of teaching is endlessly disappointing. The pupils do not seem to take the same pleasure in their tasks as she herself did, when she was a child. They do not want to spend their time copying out letters, however beautiful, for they cannot draw and they sometimes lack imagination.

She cannot understand them, and she cannot understand their lack of talent. What is wrong with them all?

Why do they find schoolwork so difficult?

Why can they not thrive in the schoolroom as she once did?

One day, she knows, she will have a pupil who shines. And in the meantime, she cares for them all, as if they were her own children.

The door swings open on its hinges.

Miss Gent looks out expectantly, but there are no children arriving. It was merely a blast of wind. She stands on the threshold and peers out, clutching her shawl to her chest. She knows it is a long journey for the children to make across the moor, many of them barefoot, or in an old pair of leather boots, two sizes too big, that has seen active service on the feet of older members of the same family.

They are poor, her pupils, used to hardship.

She scans the rise of the hill but can make out no movement beyond the flurry of snowflakes. Then, gradually, one or two dim shapes appear, and begin to make their laborious way towards the schoolhouse.

Miss Gent composes herself in readiness.

I waited too, dolefully aware my presence would be required.

It was interesting to watch her while she waited. She seemed a little apprehensive, but then I supposed she led a very lonely existence out here on the moor in her solitary schoolhouse.

It was built by the parish, at a precise location where many of the crofters' children could access it.

At last, there was the sound of muted voices outside and the wooden door scraped against the flags.

Two pinched white faces peered in, their bodies wrapped in woollen shawls, and Miss Gent greeted them.

The day could begin. The nervous waiting was over.

'Morning children. Calum. Caitlin. Please take a seat while we wait for the others.'

'I brung ma roll o' peat, Miss,' said the boy and handed it to her.

'Thank you, Calum.'

She took the fuel as payment for the lessons, and placed the dark earthy tube beside the hearth.

'Did you eat, this morning?' she asked them.

The boy nodded.

'Maw made us gruel 'fore we left.'

'Good, that's what I like to hear, Calum. You can't concentrate on an empty stomach.'

'That's what ma maw says, Miss.'

'And your maw is right, Calum.'

'She also says book learning's a waste of time, and we'd be as well stayin' home t' milk cows.'

I watched Miss Gent hesitate, the despair at her task beginning to nibble at the edges of her confidence.

Calum's little sister Caitlin just stared with her big hungry eyes, and followed Miss Gent's movements as if she was gazing at a being from another planet.

An uneasy silence fell on the schoolroom. This was one of the problems: the pupils were always arriving at different times so that it was difficult to know when to begin.

She could start the lesson, only to find herself having to go back to the beginning when new pupils arrived in dribs and drabs.

'Perhaps,' Miss Gent said, while the two children stared at her, 'while we wait for the others, we could begin by you telling me what you did this morning. Before you came here. You first, Caitlin,' she encouraged, but Caitlin looked plainly scared at being spoken to and quite unable to speak.

'Praps I'd best go first, Miss,' Calum added gently, with an air of disappointment as if his teacher had failed at the first hurdle by not anticipating Caitlin's shyness.

'Quite, Calum. You first and then we will come to you next, Caitlin.'

Calum cleared his throat and blushed slightly.

'Well, I got up early, after ma big brother Dan kicked the end of the bed, and I went outside in the dark to do ma chores.' He glanced up. 'Same as usual!'

Miss Gent nodded encouragingly, silently

acknowledging this was part of the problem with crofters' children, and one of the main reasons why they were forever nodding off before lunchtime, half-asleep at their desks, before she'd even got halfway through teaching them what they needed to know. But in the end, she supposed, all they needed to know was that you should never lose the desire to learn.

Many of the parents didn't see the value in book-learning or an education. They were never going to escape the toil of the fields anyway, and it was the soil that would give them a living in the end, not books. They owed their lives to the soil.

Miss Gent had heard it so many times before and tried not to let it dampen the fire of her enthusiasm, because once she communicated *that* to her pupils, the battle was lost.

The strength of the classroom spirit, its backbone, its belief in itself, depended on her.

'And what chores did you do?' Miss Gent asked cheerfully.

'Milked the two cows, Bessie and Charlotte, then set the fire. Brought in more peat. Fetched water.'

'I like Bessie best,' Caitlin whispered, so that only her brother could hear, but Miss Gent was encouraged by this.

'And you, Caitlin? What did you do?'

She asked the question as gently as possible.

'I made breakfast,' Caitlin hissed in a small breathy voice that barely reached the rafters. 'And helped maw with the littluns. They bain't be one year old yet.'

'The twins.'

'Aye, miss.'

Caitlin seemed completely unable to volunteer any more information and Miss Gent smiled.

'Well, let's take a look at the globe, shall we, while we wait for the others to arrive. Calum, can you fetch it?'

'Yes, miss.'

Proudly, he went to the newly-acquired learning aid and carried it carefully to their desk at the front. It spun gently on its axis.

'Now, let's see if we can find where we are on this globe.'

Caitlin stared at it, wondering if it was really possible that their own little croft with the barn and the cows, the hens and the chickens, sat somewhere on that circular coloured sphere and then she wondered how it never fell off. The child did not voice any of these concerns. She was here to learn, not ask questions. These children had this lesson drummed into them often enough on a Sunday, when the weather didn't prevent them from attending kirk with their parents.

Miss Gent began to spin the globe. 'Can you see India? Remember I told you about India last week?'

Calum's eyes lit up with excitement and for a moment Miss Gent's heart expanded and clenched. To see the hope in that bright boy's eyes, and to know that it would eventually be extinguished by the treadmill of continual poverty and hard labour on the land.

She pushed the thought down, because if she began to believe these lessons made no difference to the child, then she might as well shut up shop now, lock the door of the schoolhouse and walk away.

Every day, that winter, I witnessed her struggle in

that lonely schoolhouse on the moor, and I read her thoughts, and I read the thoughts and minds of the children gathered there, and no one saw me. I warmed my hands at the pot-bellied stove which heated the open space. I gazed out the windows, I breathed in the scent of chalk dust and leather books.

It was a peaceful, sleepy place to be. When the children nodded onto their desks with fatigue, I nodded with them, and woke up with the quick rap of Miss Gent's ruler on the desk.

The two children and the school teacher waited in the lonely schoolhouse for the other pupils to arrive, while the wind buffeted the sides of the building and set up a dismal wail in the chimney.

It felt desolate. All the elements were pitted against her schoolhouse, Miss Gent felt, like a ship at sea in a storm, and yet she liked the analogy. It amused her. Despite the solitary nature of its location, she loved the idea that all around her Nature flung itself, red in tooth and claw.

It made her feel as if there was a real battle to be fought, a real purpose in being here.

Voices carried on the air and Calum and Caitlin at the front desks lifted their heads to listen. The patter of little feet, high-pitched calls, snatched away by the wind, then the door was flung open once again. More ruddy windswept faces, wrapped in shawls, bare muddied feet, thick-soled leather boots with holes in them, clogs, threadbare clothes, worn and mended, the crust of dirt recently brushed off them.

'Come and warm yourselves by the fire, children,' Miss Gent told them, at the sight of their bare icy feet.

Once they were all settled at their desks, the morning lessons could begin.

Miss Gent enjoyed this part of the day.

She did not enjoy the waiting, the anticipation of their arrival, but once they were all together under her roof, and she was in the swing of the first lesson, she got into her stride and found that time swept past in a merry whirl of occupation and industry. Little incidents would amuse her; the sight of their faces, wide-eyed, full of wonder at the mystery of the world, kept her entertained and warmed her heart.

At the end of the day, Miss Gent stood at the door and watched the children begin their long trek back to their homes, across the moor.

She tucked little Caitlin's hair into her cap, and fastened her shawl tighter. Calum and Caitlin – her favourites!

As she watched them walk away, she looked up at the sky wonderingly. Would they still make the journey when it snowed? Such a long walk for many of them.

She turned back into the schoolhouse and warmed her hands at the stove.

Still she did not see me in the corner. The rest of her day was her own, but it would be long and empty. She began to busy herself about the range, to make herself a cup of tea and boil an egg.

Chickens clucked in the coop outside, sheltered from the worst of the weather. A goat was tethered in the barn, and these creatures had become Miss Gent's companions over the last few months, since arriving here. They gave her sustenance and she gave them love, of a sort.

She ate a frugal meal, wrapped herself up against the cold, changed into thick winter boots and went outside. She lifted her face to the wind and sniffed the horizon. There was pleasure on her face.

She would enjoy a brisk afternoon walk across the moors. The village was not far, maybe half an hour on foot? Perhaps she would go there. Call on the minister, he who had organized this school in the first place. They always had much to chat about.

She set off quite happily, head bent to the wind, minding herself to hurry back before dusk fell.

While she was away, the schoolhouse sat in silence. And I sat within it. Restless. Wondering. Crossing the bare boards, I touched the globe with an outstretched finger and watched it spin. The Ottoman Empire, Constantinople, countries and empires – from my perspective – become so quickly out of date.

The next morning, at first light, Miss Gent prepared herself for another day. She got the schoolroom ready, kept the stove burning, and glanced out the window.

Calum and Caitlin were always first to arrive, but there was no sign of their two little figures on the horizon this morning.

She kept looking, but still they did not come. Even after the other pupils had arrived, their desks remained ominously empty.

I knew why, of course, but I could not break the news to her. I was invisible. She did not see me, she did not even sense me, although one or two of the poorer children glanced nervously towards the back of the classroom where I stood, as if something troubled them.

Miss Gent did not receive the news that day. She continued to wait for them, and when they did not arrive, she hid her disappointment and worry from the other children.

She listened to the chesty coughs of the youngsters, noted the heightened colour of their cheeks, and persistently ignored my presence in the corner of the room, for what good would it do, in the end, to see me standing there? How would that help?

Next day dawned, and after her early chores were finished, she swept the little schoolhouse in readiness. There was a flurry of snowflakes on the air, she could see from the window, and then there was a knock at the door.

When it creaked open, it was to her great relief that she saw their two little faces, looking up at her from their black wrappings of knitted shawl.

She looked over their heads into the continuing snowfall.

'You're the first. Again.'

'We're always the first,' Calum whispered, and in they came, to Miss Gent's profound relief. Safe and well. Saved from the peril of whatever fever had felled them.

For many days Calum and Caitlin were her only pupils.

'How is it,' she asked them, 'that you can manage to reach me through the snow, when the others can't?'

She asked the question fondly, but they did not reply.

And so it went on, every morning for a week, even as the snow fell outside.

In the afternoons, the children left and dusk came down.

When the snow would allow, the minister visited. He – surely, considering his profession – would notice me hovering by the window? His sombre attire was black as death itself, but he did not once glance in my direction. A little offended, I touched the globe next to me and made it softly spin.

He did turn then, but only briefly, and with a slightly puzzled, distracted air.

Then his attention was focused entirely on Miss Gent, to whom he had some distressing news to impart.

I watched her struggle with the emotions she fought to hide. Her shawl was crossed precisely at the front and tied at the back, with careful discipline. She was neat and trim, as ever, but her shoulders sagged.

She waited until the minister had left before she began to weep.

Calum and Caitlin – her favourite pupils – would be absent from the classroom from now on. Their little desks at the front empty, their hopes and dreams for a better future forever quenched. There would be no more learning for the bright-eyed Calum and his shy little sister.

They were gone.

I already knew that – of course.

I had been called away in the night one week earlier, found myself at the cabin where Calum and Caitlin lived, where their parents scraped a meagre living off the land.

Fevers were sudden in the cold winter months. They could fell you in an hour.

Caitlin had not risen from her bed that first morning. Calum was the next to succumb.

They lingered in and out of delirium. Their father sent for the doctor, but he had a more important client to deal with – the laird's daughter had fallen sick. By the time he arrived at their humble cabin, it was too late.

It is not a particularly remarkable story. Then, as now, the poorest and the weakest are the first to suffer.

It was a day or two later that she thought to ask the Reverend Mackay the exact date of their deaths. When he told her, she stared at him, but did not say what was on her mind.

The children had been visiting the schoolhouse for several days after they were supposed to be lying in the ground. A week in fact. Every morning, turning up regular as clockwork, long before the other pupils arrived.

'Well, good day, Miss Gent,' Reverend Mackay said.

'Good day,' Miss Gent replied.

Neither of them mentioned what they were thinking. Ghost and ghouls do not inhabit strict Presbyterian communities in the highlands of Scotland, where rules are strictly followed and adhered to. There is no margin to allow the darkness through. Miss Gent's neatness keeps the darkness from coming inside.

My smile in the shadows gives me away. Once again, I set that globe spinning, and this time she half-turns her head.

And with that, I abandon poor Miss Gent to her fate, with the wind still buffeting the schoolhouse walls. I am reluctant to leave her there, but leave her there I must.

The Youth of Yesterday

I am often asked, who do you most regret working with?

That's easy to answer.

The young. The hopeful Youth of Today who believe they can change the world – and die trying to. They so quickly become the Youth of Yesterday.

I am thinking of a manufactured tent city in a vast public square in China, a generation of students who set up their flimsy shelters temporarily and refused to budge, in a bid to force change. One image in particular became iconic, and footage of it can still be seen today. A slim youth, with a white flag in his hands, standing in the path of oncoming tanks, defying the military might of China with nothing but a t-shirt on his back and a flag of peace in his hand. He stood up to them, refused to move. The foolhardy courage of the young. He raised his arms high above his head, stood with his chest out, and dared them to crush him, while all the world's media were watching.

And this, of course, they dared not do. Not while all the world's media were watching.

He stood with his foot on the tread, and when they made as if to swerve and move aside, he moved too and cut off their path again. A defenceless, unarmed youth with no body armour, no weaponry, no power, no status, nothing but himself and his will to challenge the powers that be. And it disarmed the might of China for a brief moment in history. All the machinery of war could not defy that iconic symbol of freedom of expression.

Days later I walked that tent city where the students had set up camp. They were united in their desire for change. They genuinely believed they could change the world: that China, like Russia, was ready for change, and would submit to the will of the people. The Berlin Wall had yet to be dismantled, brick by brick, by ordinary citizens.

There was a powerful sense of camaraderie among the students as they sat before their camp stoves, sharing small bowls of hot food, talking, singing, aware they were creating a moment in history that would never be forgotten. Although it is forgotten, in China at least. No one is allowed to refer to it, and I have reason to believe no one now left remembers. Their collective memory wiped clean, in an efficient manner of slow corrosion, and years of silence and obedience.

I found the young boy among the crowd, the one who had been foolish enough to step out into the path of the tanks and make a fool of them all. Fragile human being, pitted against machine.

He was there among them, laughing in a group. At night they lay in their sleeping bags under the stars, and when the soldiers and the tanks lined up, they still refused to move. The Chinese government and the military would not dare, not while all the world's press were watching. But as soon as the gaze of the world was turned elsewhere, the tanks began to edge forward like metal monsters and, incredibly, they rolled over the rows and rows of sleeping and supine students, crushing them where they lay. The tanks did not stop. They slaughtered and they slaughtered, and the foolish young man was slaughtered alongside them. And those who remained alive at the end of the day were incarcerated, locked up, never to be seen again.

Their hopes and dreams had come to nothing, after such a promising start. And I had to bear witness, as all the world bore witness and has never forgotten. But it was I who had to ferry each one from that desolate square with its makeshift tents, and see them safely on their way. It drained me, for I – alone of you all – had known all along what was coming.

I am not granted the privilege of hope, because all too often I am already familiar with the end story. I know what will happen, what will become of your noble youth with the fire for change in their bellies, how it will end. And it pains me to know it.

That square in China was a place I will never return to. The cries, the weeping, the unforgettable sights… that is not something I ever want to revisit.

And that is not all.

I have seen walking skeletons, starving in a world of plenty. I have seen children mown down by the march of politics and history. I have seen famine and flood, families clinging to their corrugated-tin roofs, losing everything, their children, their lives.

I have watched it all. Storm, flood, disease, conflict, battle, starvation, revolution.

It does not matter if you or your friends knew their names, or if no one knew them. It's not just a numbers game, you see. I lose count. How could I possibly keep a tally? It is not possible. But not one single life is forgotten – not by me.

'Do you ever wish you were one of us?'

I look at her and smile.

'You?' I reply. 'Never! I mean, look at the perks of the job!'

I am lying, of course.

I wish I were human. I would like to be part of your struggling sea of humanity, with your love and pain, your grasp of ideas and your tragic inability to get things right. I wish I were one of you.

I am not allowed to give up, to rest, to concede defeat. And I have no way of knowing how long this journey will last, if there will ever be an end to it.

I never take centre stage. I am always in the wings, watching. Leonard beckoned me because he knew I was there, but I was too shy to step forward. It would not be appropriate, I told him. You take the limelight; it is yours, after all.

You have so much to fear, and yet so much to be thankful for.

Many is the time I have slipped into a dismal little sitting-room with a gas fire and a sense of time warp, as if the occupant is stuck in the 1950s, or 1960s perhaps, and have found an ageing relative there, left alone, watching the clock tick inexorably forward, with no one to watch it with her. A childless woman sitting in a desolate, friendless city somewhere in Middle England. The curtains opposite twitch. Neighbours look out for her, because they know there is no remaining family to beat a path to her door. She leaves it unlocked, against the advice of her carers, although she is mainly chair-ridden. She tells them she prefers to leave it unlocked because she does not want her guests to feel unwelcome. She wants to welcome the outside world in. She sits in shawls with the TV turned up too loud, and the remote control in her hand, and flicks through channels and has a valid, rational opinion on any subject in town. Putin, Theresa May, Jeremy Corbyn, the exit from the EU and what an unfortunate state of affairs that will be. She is modern, in touch: she voted Remain in the referendum. It is only her body which fails her.

She has the radio on a stool beside her armchair, and knows exactly when to adjust the dial to find *The Archers*, those comfortable voices which lead her by the hand into the village of Ambridge. *Woman's Hour, Book at Bedtime*, the world comes to Beryl through the airwaves, and she is never cut off from the great events of life. She was born in the 1920s and was a teenager during the Second World War, remembers hunkering down in the Anderson shelter and watching her respectable, genteel mother consume half a bottle of whisky, riven by worry for her eldest daughter who was out at the cinema in town somewhere, and had not returned since the air raid began.

Beryl has seen the start of the Cold War, the rolling out of the Iron Curtain, the Wall being built, brick by brick, and then torn down again twenty-eight years later. She has seen governments and ideologies rise and fall, her finger on the dial, her gaze out the window, through the drift of net curtain up to the clouds above.

She fills her lonely front room with noise from

the world, as it comforts her, and has comforted her throughout her childless older years.

A carer visits twice a day, whose services she pays dearly for. They dress her in the morning and leave a sandwich for her supper under a plate. Meals on wheels arrives at noon, with a hot meal under a metal lid. At six in the evening, another stranger arrives to undress her and she tries to talk to them about her nieces and nephew but they are not particularly interested. They are underpaid, running late. Some of them are kind. Beryl doesn't like it if a stranger appears, just when she'd got used to the lovely little girl from Bengal. (In fact, she is 44, but to Beryl, in her ninety-sixth year, she is a child still).

The house was built in 1951 and the stairs are steep. But Beryl hangs onto the banister and pulls herself up every night like Chris Bonington conquering Everest. She was forced to have a spell in hospital recently, and the doctors advised she would not be allowed home until she could walk again. They said she would never manage the stairs, but Beryl proved them wrong.

Her sitting room was waiting for her with its voices from the world echoing through the ether. She had events to catch up on, a routine to slip back into.

No one is ready to die.

If they say they are, it's a lie.

Hitler's Bunker

'Well, that's all so fascinating,' Marcia murmurs, and her enthusiasm is a little too bright, a little too plastic. Her teeth glint in the sharp light, like a fox. I can see her attention is wavering.

'I could tell you about Hitler's Bunker?' I suggest.

'Could you? You were there, of course?'

I shrug without saying anything. Of course I was there. I am everywhere.

Her eyebrows lift in anticipation. I have her hooked.

Hitler's demise is always a good one. Who doesn't want to see the end of him?

I can take her there, back through the decades, to the moment when Europe was torn apart by war, and ordinary Berliners were desperate and broken.

And of Hitler? Well, he was hiding underground, like the rat he was, and other rats lurked there with him.

And just like that, I take her there, to the underground chambers he occupied in his last days.

There were a few of them, in that concrete system of tunnels buried deep beneath the wartime streets of Berlin. I stalked the corridors. They had meeting rooms, offices, bedrooms, luxurious bathrooms with all the latest gadgetry of the day. Bombs shuddered in the distance. I hated being trapped down there with them, but I had no choice.

I knew what was coming, and I suspect so did they.

They knew they were finished. The Russians were advancing in one direction, the Americans in the other, and bombs had destroyed most of the city streets, leaving the few survivors destitute and homeless. Children lived like rats in cellars and ruins – scavengers. There was no bunker built for them, safe from bombs.

They talked of suicide all the time. It was a polite topic of conversation at the dinner table, knives scraping against the best china, port glinting in crystal glasses, because they knew by now that the Russians were only a few miles away.

It was the children that upset me.

They lied to them, of course, told them Uncle Adolf was a hero, and the Third Reich would last a thousand years.

Magda Goebbels. Her eyes full of unfathomable darkness.

She hero-worshipped her husband and their leader. She would go with him wherever he led, into terrible darkness if need be.

When the artillery sounded in the distance she told the children it was thunder. Only the eldest, Hilde, did not believe her.

I don't really want to talk about that... the way she put them to bed that night.

She handed them their bedtime drink, which all of them drank except Hilde, who complained it tasted funny. She watched her siblings being encouraged to drink it, and she noticed the odd intensity of her mother.

She stared at the adults suspiciously. I was standing

in the corner of the room when Magda came to say goodnight to them, but Hilde was sulky. She refused to look at her mother.

When Magda grew angry and said, 'You will drink it, Hilde!' the girl turned her face to the wall. Her mother dragged her by the shoulders, bent her head, and made her swallow. Some of the milk spilled down her chin and onto her nightdress and was wasted.

When the child at last looked up, she saw me standing there. We locked eyes for the briefest of moments and I hated myself. None of this is my doing, I wanted to cry. She recognized me for what I was. As she climbed into the bunk beside her brother and sisters, she protested sleepily. Her mother, Magda – she with murder in her eyes – did not glance at me once. That woman was the engineer of her own children's fate. She left me with nothing to do but stare in horror at what you humans in your madness are capable of.

I stood there a long time, while the concrete corridors shuddered and echoed to the boom of the artillery above, bombs scooping out craters that grew nearer and nearer.

I was busy that night, and many nights before it.

But this I remember.

A mother slipping back into the room where her children lay sleeping after lights out, and pushing a cyanide capsule between the teeth of each one, listening for the crunch as she closed their jaw upon it. She was business-like and efficient. But when she got to the last, Hilde was awake. They looked at each other. The little girl struggled, so there was a terrible undignified moment when mother and daughter fought, until

Magda prevailed. She clamped her daughter's jaw so hard between her white knuckles that I heard the bone snap. She broke Hilde's jaw in her effort to get the 'medicine' down her daughter's throat.

And then they lay there, in that chamber of death. Five little bodies in the bunks, all tumbled together. And the bombs still rained down from the sky, and Magda appeared to smile upon her handiwork, like a good mother putting her children to bed for one last time.

I am used to seeing many sights in my line of work, but even I could not help shuddering.

I wanted to escape that cold bunker as quickly as I could.

I don't really remember what Magda Goebbels was wearing. Probably pearls and high heels, as always.

The Theatre of War

I don't like to admit this to Marcia and her readers, but sometimes there is a lust for blood which sits at odds with my better feelings.

Other than birth, death is the single most momentous event in the life of any human being, and it is my duty to lock eyes with the victim and let them know I am there: that this is the moment of reckoning.

Sometimes, they are snatched away from me at the last, and when this happens I breathe a genuine sigh of relief. I have hovered above operating tables before now while the flesh is pinned back, exposing a scarlet chest cavity, pulsing with life, and the machines have bleeped, and the surgeons have panicked, but remained focused on their job – as I must perform mine – and so often it is the surgeons who are victorious. We fight a crude battle without weapons in that theatre. The Theatre of War. And either they win or I win, in the end.

I must confess I don't make a habit of fighting very hard in this particular context. I am rooting always for the opposition, with their surgical knives, tiny glinting implements which carve and sever with such delicate precision. Sometimes the blood level drops, the pulse slows, and the heart monitor stops bleeping, and then I know it will be my turn to step forward from the shadows. The patient will sit up on the operating table, leave their fleshy body behind and walk with me, away from the screaming monitors and the panic and pandemonium that ensues beneath the glare of the light. And quite often we will pause in the corridor outside and observe the relatives – if there are any – anxiously waiting for news. One of them will invariably have his head in his hands, one – a well-meaning friend – will be offering cups of tea from the self-service machine – another will be in shock.

But mostly nowadays, I am delighted to inform you, I walk away the loser, particularly after a routine operation. Such are the improvements of modern medicine. Although, let's not beat about the bush, you're never going to eliminate me completely. I get you all in the end, one way or another.

I am strangely captivated during these operations. I peer over their shoulders, these heroic women and men of medicine, and watch the finesse with which they work. I watch their sharp little blades glinting, swift and sure. I watch the inner-workings of the body – so mechanically beautiful, a feat of engineering, tidy, flawlessly designed. Every sentient body, even that of a mouse, is an engine running on its own fuel. A work of art. A ticking mechanism like a clock.

Tick tock...

Tick tock...

Tick tock...

until it stops...

I revel in it, celebrate its beauty and perfection, even with all the ugliness of decay that goes on.

Don't get me wrong, I'm as squeamish as the next person. I used to have a particular phobia about hospitals, their corridors filled with shuffling half-corpses, the living and the barely-living, struggling on crutches with bags of fluid and blood attached to them. The smokers at the entrance, puffing away the last of their oxygen even while waiting for limbs to be amputated due to poor circulation.

I used to dread them as places of death and decay.

Me! Afraid of hospitals!

Then I started to observe the operations and became lost in the finer workings of the surgeon's skill. I do admire their ability to keep such a steady hand, a focused eye, while all the time ignoring the shadow of *Yours Truly* standing in the corner.

Tick tock...

Tick tock...

Tock...

Of course, the mortuaries are full to overflowing. To harvest such a bumper crop as that is not a pleasant business. It becomes too routine, mechanical, like a conveyor belt.

They keep them in steel drawers nowadays like some kind of macabre filing cabinet, tags of identification on their toes. Like homing pigeons, except they will never come home.

It's a bit like a library with an index and a cataloguing system, but instead of books, you've got bodies.

Who could envy my line of work?

Who would want to shoulder my burden, perform my task, day after day, night after night, for centuries without end?

'And yet – you look good on it,' Marcia interjects.

She's right. I'm the picture of health. It's almost an insult. That's why you don't always recognize me. I pride myself on my good looks and always have lipstick to hand. A quick dash of coral pink and I'm as good as new: hair washed, cheeks glowing with rude health.

So when I come upon fresh young blood, it hurts to be there at the kill but I have no choice.

It is my duty.

And I do it well.

Where do You Begin and End?

'We've talked a lot about some of your cases, but can you tell us a little bit about yourself?' Marcia suggests now. 'Give our readers some context. Where were you born, that kind of thing.'

Rather a bizarre question to ask me, I feel.

'Apart from the fact I don't like hospitals you mean?'

My gaze fixes on the window, where I can just make out the bulky mass of the Castle rearing out of its black rock. That rock is now polished by a recent rainfall and gleams ebony. Time slows down, unfolds and elongates like a linen sheet on which everything is spread.

'To be honest, I don't really know when it all began. I suppose I've been here for as long as humanity has. Where you walked, I followed. Across continents, into the Northern darkness.'

A vision pops into my head of five slender figures walking across an immense plain, a trail of them, divided by space. Not speaking to each other, just slowly continuing their journey through mist, glimpsed from a distance, when this little planet spinning in space was barely populated.

I would like to give Marcia an accurate description of my own beginnings, my provenance, but it is not within my power.

'The truth is,' I tell her, 'I don't remember.'

She looks at me, disappointed.

'I arrived, and then I was here. In Space and Time, but outside of it too.'

No matter how hard Marcia tries, she cannot quite get her head round it. She aims for a light-hearted tone that completely eludes us. We keep finding ourselves washed up in unfamiliar backwaters, full of dangerous undercurrents which threaten to drag us into the open and expose us.

'Let me tell you another story,' I soothe her.

And she listens, like a child.

Topliffe Hall
(or Two Birds with One Stone)

'Do you believe in ghosts?' Marcia asks me.

'Now, there's a question,' I reply. 'And quite a knotty one. I can tell you a little ghost story, if you like, about a haunted block of apartments, where the elderly residents often hear a baby crying in the night. Footsteps have been heard on the stairs, but when they look, the staircase is empty: no grandchildren have been reported visiting the place, either. Certainly no babies.'

Marcia's eyes widen with excitement.

'How intriguing,' she says.

'Been going on for years. It's a mansion block called Topliffe Hall, near Hampstead Heath. You might have heard of it?'

Marcia pauses and shakes her head. 'Not that I know of.'

'That's strange,' I venture.

'Why?' she asks.

'Oh, no reason,' I smile evasively, but there is a reason, of course. She may not have heard of it – yet – but her own mother will live there one day, in that mansion block, and she too will hear the wailing infant, which others have heard, and for Marcia's mother it will be a painful reminder of her own daughter's birth – and her loss.

But of course Marcia does not know any of this yet, and I am in no hurry to enlighten her.

'Topliffe Hall,' I tell her, 'a hundred or so years ago, used to be on the outskirts of London, out in the countryside, long before the city swamped it. Interesting how your urban sprawl transforms a place. Wind the clock back a century or two and you find yourself standing in open fields, with the morning dew pearling the landscape.'

I smile to myself contentedly at the visions afforded to me.

'I am a traveller in time, and it is fascinating, absolutely fascinating.'

She nods appreciatively.

'I thought you said you were suffering from fatigue?'

'Yes, I'm tired, Marcia, but even so, is it a crime to take pleasure in some of my memories?'

'No, of course not!'

'So, back to the story. Before Topliffe Hall was divided into luxury apartments, it was a grand residence.'

'And a grand family lived there?'

'Well,' I hesitate. 'Not quite. Let me introduce you to Helen De'Ath.'

'De'Ath?' Marcia asks, incredulously.

'Yes, that's right. De'Ath.'

And I continue:

'She was seventeen years old when she arrived at Topliffe Hall.'

'Mmm… sounds like a fairy tale,' Marcia murmurs.

'It's no fairy tale, I'm afraid.'

The carriage turned abruptly to the right, and Helen

felt the change of pace on her journey out of London from her father's house. I was sitting beside her, of course, even then, and watched her closely. Strictly speaking, we were dealing with a birth rather than a death, but I was hovering close by, just the same. It looked like we were in for the long haul.

Helen pulled the drape aside and saw the broad sweep of a gravel driveway, curving round to a massive stone façade, like something out of a Jane Austen novel. Row upon row of windows glinting in the evening light. The sun came out briefly and as it did so, she saw clouds moving across the windowpanes.

You might have thought our heroine would be pretty delighted to arrive at such an address, but this wasn't a social call, and she knew it.

The building was three storeys high and extremely long, with turrets along the roofline. It was grand, elegant, as if once made for a different purpose other than the one it now served.

A wide stone staircase swept up to the entrance. Figures appeared to attend to the horses, and Helen was escorted up the steps. I followed her and stood aside to observe. No one noticed me, of course.

'Perhaps they thought you were a servant?' Marcia chimes in, pleased with her own interpretation.

'Possibly,' and I give a tight smile.

I don't like being interrupted, mid-flow.

Everyone appeared to know their place, have a job to perform.

Helen waited passively for what might happen next.

In the hallway, which was floored with marble, there stood a desk with a large ledger on it, and a quill pen. There were gas lamps on the walls, a recent innovation. Nurses in grey starched uniforms passed through the foyer from time to time.

'She has no possessions with her.'

They were talking about her in the third person.

No one addressed her personally, something which both she and I noticed.

Her sense of isolation was, I could tell, increasing.

'You will come this way please.'

Helen hesitated, then did as she was told.

She had no choice.

I followed, stumbling after her, invisible I hoped.

In the office Helen was ordered to take off her cloak. She felt chilly without it, vulnerable.

'My name is Mrs Foreman,' said a woman with a hard face, 'and this – as you will be aware – is Topliffe Hall.'

'I know. My father has spoken about it often.'

'We dislike our patients speaking out of turn here. You will soon learn that. There are lots of girls here like you.'

'Like me?'

I do a quick double-take, glancing first at the old harridan behind the desk, then at Miss De'Ath, our heroine.

'Patients?' I declare out loud, and Mrs Foreman's eyes suddenly fix on me, as if she can actually see me.

She blinks, then looks away. Helen remains oblivious.

'If you behave yourself you will be allowed to take classes in sewing. There are lots of pursuits to interest you – if you have a mind to obey. Occupation is good for the soul, prevents all kinds of moral decay. There are lots of interesting people here.'

None of this sounds good, but when Helen is dismissed from the office, I leave alongside her, shadowing my charge. I realise it is my duty, for the moment, to go whither she does.

'What does she mean by interesting?' I hear Helen ask one of the other girls, later.

'She means mad.'

There are two rows of beds along each side of the dormitory.

Twelve beds in all.

No one spoke to Helen, except Meg. The others were moon-faced and silent.

'There's been some kind of mistake,' Helen tried to explain. 'I shouldn't really be here.'

I watched Meg nod sympathetically.

'That's what they all say, at first. You'd be amazed how many mistakes are made. It will be nice to have someone to talk to.'

When the girls are ordered to the washroom Helen falls into line behind Meg, and I fall into line behind Helen, while a nurse appears at the door, barking orders.

'That's right. Nice and gently now.'

We all walk in line to the washroom where a row of cold baths awaits.

I decide to step aside at that point. I don't much like getting wet, at least not like that. A hot bath in a good hotel is acceptable, but not this.

I watched poor Helen struggle while they wrenched the gown from her shoulders.

'There's been some kind of mistake. I shouldn't be here.'

The nurses in uniform ignored her, as two of them forced her into a wooden tub shaped like a coffin. It took me a moment to realise it was packed with ice. They closed a wooden lid over it so that only her head stuck out, then the patients were left there all in a row, nailed in. Like living corpses with their heads sticking out.

I couldn't believe it.

After half an hour they let them out again, so cold they were subdued as if by torture. I couldn't intervene. I just had to watch.

As they put a gown back over her head, I heard Helen say, 'Does my father know I'm here?'

'He must do, dearie. He's the one who sent you here.'

'It's always the husbands or the fathers,' another remarked.

Nurses in starched caps spoke to each other, but not to Helen.

Ah, I thought, so that's what this place is.

Somewhere to send the daughters who have misbehaved, embarrassed the family.

The sewing room where she worked by day was cold and her fingers were stiff. The only time she was warm was when she slipped under the sheets at night, and even then the draughts crept along the floorboards and whistled through the dormitory.

I expect she often thought about her father's study, its warm crimson carpet and the glowing hearth, while she waited anxiously for him to visit.

Mrs Foreman was a vociferous old boot. I stood listening while she lectured the poor inmates.

'Useful and gainful employment is the perfect antidote for the minds of degenerate young females. That's the philosophy of Topliffe Hall.'

And on another occasion: 'We hold up a mirror to our souls. Now we see through a glass darkly, then we shall see face to face.'

The girls were set to stitch religious samplers, biblical texts, along the themes of obedience, chastity and domesticity. Helen thought about other words she would like to stitch instead. Words like explosion or cataclysm or vibrant or bejewelled. But these were no longer part of the vocabulary of the girls of Topliffe Hall. A whole new lexicon applied now.

They sat at the long refectory tables on benches like schoolgirls, and the scrape of spoons against bowls was the only sound. Nurses monitored their movements like prison guards, keeping an eye out for any trouble.

Helen glanced along the row at a girl called Eliza Turnbull, who sat there, not eating.

Eliza was a sad case indeed. She had not spoken in many years. She was dressed in a high-necked black dress with a white collar.

'What's wrong with her?' Helen whispered to Meg.

'She was the only servant in a big house,' Meg whispered back. I sat on the bench beside them, leaning forward so I could hear.

'They worked her so hard that by the time she had finished lighting and attending to the last fireplace in the house, she had to start all over again. Exhausted, poor thing! A house with twenty rooms. They were too mean to employ any other servants to help her. That's how she ended up in here. She doesn't eat. Sometimes they have to force-feed her.'

'Rise!' one of the nurses commanded.

I watched as the girls rose, and stood up behind their benches, then filed out of the room in single file.

On the way back to the dormitory there was a commotion. A scuffle, a scream, the whack of a stick coming down sharply. I thought about intervening, but it was not my place to.

More screaming. Raised voices.

Two of the nurses had hold of Eliza firmly by the arms.

'What's wrong?' Helen asked.

'She tried to hurt herself again,' Meg told her. 'She threw herself against the door jamb. She's always trying to injure herself.'

'How long is she here for?' Helen asked.

Meg looked back at her in disbelief.

I noticed that look, although neither of them noticed me.

Helen was summoned to the doctor's office, and of course I shuffled along with her, discreet as ever. Discretion is my middle name.

'Is it?' Marcia interjects.

I look at her sourly. 'No. I'm joking.'

To continue…

'I have been looking at your case notes, Helen. We have a diagnosis. Your father is very satisfied with our efforts.'

Doctor Hughes looked up from his thick ledger.

'It is much easier once we have a diagnosis, you see. Gives us something to work with.'

'And what is my… diagnosis?'

'Hysteria and insanity, caused by over-excitement of the brain.'

He thwacked his black ledger shut with a bang, and a cloud of dust lifted in the air. 'Too many ideas! Too much thinking!'

He lay a heavy hand on the black leather binding and for a moment Helen had the notion it contained all of their sins and misdemeanours. Mrs Foreman stood to attention against one wall, conceding to the doctor's male superiority.

'There are ways to treat you, Helen. And we have been following procedures for best practice.'

Helen opened her mouth to speak, but Mrs Foreman stepped forward, and cut her off. 'It is not your place to question, Helen, but merely to endure. And to obey. So that we can make you better. HOWEVER, we have encountered a new problem. One of your own making.'

Mrs Foreman pursed her lips.

'Your father will have to be informed, of course. Well, you wouldn't be the first – and you certainly won't be the last.'

So, therein lay the problem.

Well, I had to leave Helen there at Topliffe Hall for a while. I had duties elsewhere. But when I returned, things had moved on apace. As the weeks and months slid by for Helen, the evidence began to show even through the looseness of her gown.

'There must be some mistake,' she kept repeating.

'Is that right, dearie?'

No one listened to her.

I watched as the other girls began to show an interest. Meg, in particular, asked lots of questions.

'What does it feel like?' she whispered.

Helen lay on her back, and looked up at the skylight above her bed. Even I could see that the light was different, softer, brighter. Snowflakes were slowly drifting through the sky and landing softly on the windowpane.

At that moment, the baby kicked inside her. I felt it. She felt it. It's so strange the way I can feel things sometimes.

'It feels like a bird, trapped inside me,' Helen said out loud, and I nodded at that.

Seemed like a good description, but no one paid me any heed. I began to wonder myself what it might feel like, to have that privilege, a little bud of life uncurling inside you. What must it be like to create life, rather than to stand guard at the threshold, and usher the sad souls on their way?

I watched as she waited for a visit from her father, but she waited in vain.

She gazed longingly at the line of trees beyond the lawn. Dark stripes against the white of the snow. I wonder if she ever thought of vanishing there, running away so that no one would find her?

Whenever she showed too much pleasure in her condition, holding the dome of her belly in a protective manner like any expectant mother, one of the nurses would sneer at her, 'Do you really think they'll let you keep it?'

White days of silence followed, snow landing on the lawn, where they were never allowed to walk.

She became as heavy as a drum, ponderous with her great burden.

At night she dreamt about Doctor Hughes' visits to her father's house – visits which had grown more frequent as she grew older. He was the one who had signed the certificate to ensure Helen had a place here at Topliffe Hall. She remembered his oily tones, his hand resting on her knee like a spider.

She dreamt she was trapped in a dolls' house where all the people around her were made of plaster.

'It is only a dream,' she told herself, as she stared in horror at the face of the doll standing next to her.

It was meant to resemble her father, but she had been here so long she was beginning to forget what he looked like.

Then she woke to the chill of the dormitory, the snufflings of the other sleeping girls, the rustle of rough sheets, a cough from Anne, whose bed was too near the door.

I checked my watch.

This particular assignment was proving to be more time-consuming than I had bargained for, but I was prepared to stay the course. I had to.

Although I didn't really know why.

*

'The Devil is in you, child. You must pray for forgiveness.'

Mrs Foreman was very clear on that point, and instructed the nurses to be clear too.

She was in the sewing room when her waters broke. A stream of hot liquid hit the floor with a warm surprise. No one had told her to expect this. Helen turned to one of the nurses she had taken to calling Hatchet-Face when no one but Meg was about to hear. And *Yours Truly*, of course.

'What shall I do now?'

'Not a lot you can do. You'll be hours yet. And it will hurt like hell. That's if you survive!'

'Don't listen to her,' Meg said, putting an arm around Helen's shoulder.

Helen wished her friend could stay with her but Hatchet-Face was already calling over one of the other nurses to help.

'Come on,' they instructed.

'Where?' Helen asked.

'Where are you taking her?' I demanded, although no one paid me any heed.

They propelled her towards the door, and I scuttled after them, along a series of grey corridors until we finally arrived in a room dismal with stains, and cold.

A high bed awaited her.

Like an altar.

A place of sacrifice.

Helen shuddered at the sight. And I'm really not surprised at that.

'Don't worry. I'm here,' I reassured her, feeling motherly all of a sudden, but Helen blanked me, for– despite her name, and her destiny – she knew nothing of me.

Hatchet-Face slapped the high bench.

'Get yourself up there,' she commanded.

Helen did as she was told.

'You'll need to wait.'

'What for?'

'For a midwife or a doctor?' I interjected hopefully, but they blanked me again.

'For the pains to start.'

Then they left her.

They abandoned her in that stark cell, leaving her to wait for the baby to arrive.

But it didn't, of course. Babies don't turn up just like that, not before a lot of caterwauling and pain, anyway.

The room was bare and lacked any kind of adornment, apart from a wooden and ivory crucifix high on one wall. It loomed over Helen with little compassion.

What she felt was judged, condemned. There was so much unnecessary detail in that image. Nails were driven into the gory feet, cream-coloured toes were bent with imaginary pain, twisted and contorted out of shape until they no longer resembled toes at all, but fingers. An effigy of pain.

Helen felt sick.

Her mind looped in circles.

No one came, even when she began to cry.

The first wave of pain bore down on her, and I coached

her through it, clutching her hand, although of course she couldn't feel it.

'Take deep breaths. Concentrate. Relax.'

I was well outside my remit. I'm often present at births, hovering there just in case. It's a twin portal, after all. You never really know which way it's going to swing.

But I'm only on standby. I try not to get involved.

But I felt quite attached to Helen De'Ath. Maybe it was the name. I don't know.

An hour later and the pain was more intense.

She was still alone, and growing more frightened by the minute.

When she called for help, no one heard her, and her voice echoed back at her from the drab walls.

She began to suspect them of dubious motives, and I must admit, I did too.

Let her perish – and the unwanted child alongside her. No one would be any the wiser. One less waif and stray to worry about. Kill two birds with one stone.

On hearing receding footsteps in the corridor beyond, she filled her lungs with air and shouted for help, as loudly as she could. But, unbelievably, they ignored her.

We heard them walking away, the slap of a distant door swinging shut.

Then again – silence.

'Don't worry. It'll be okay. We're in this together,' I urged, but it was no use.

She was crawling off the high bed and down onto

the cold floor like an animal when the footsteps came running.

Voices.

Arms gripping her from behind, levering her back onto the high bed.

'Now, now. Back you go,' someone commanded.

'She's never going to survive this.'

'She'll lose that baby.'

This verdict seemed to spur her on to greater efforts, and she clawed her way into position.

The battle was long and hard, and I confess I had to look away on more than one occasion. Birth isn't really my area, you know.

One last monumental push and she was ripped asunder.

A wet creature flopped onto the shore beside her, covered in blood and mucus, attached by a thick rippling snake of crimson flesh. I saw Helen stare at this in horror, and realised that probably no one had told her about the umbilical cord. She had never seen one before.

Breathless, Helen reached out her arms to receive her child.

Hatchet-Face wasn't present, for once, and one of the nurses lay the child on her breast while they cut the cord.

'It's a girl,' she was told.

'I shall call her Hetty.'

At first she thought no one had heard her, but I saw one of the nurses give her a sympathetic glance.

'You'll call her nothing,' another barked. 'It's for her parents to name her.'

'Parents? But I am her—'

'Didn't they make that one clear, dearie? It's the orphanage for this one. If she's lucky she'll be adopted by a nice middle-class family who can afford to keep her.'

'I can afford to keep her.'

'Not anymore you can't. Not without your father's support.'

'But he—'

'—is nowhere to be seen. He's disowned you, girl. Don't you get it?'

The kinder of the two nurses placed a restraining hand on the other one's arm.

'Please, there's no need to—'

'No need to what? Tell her the truth? Sooner she knows the better, is my opinion.'

She was allowed to hold Hetty for a few moments.

The little girl was cleaned and wrapped in a blanket – not a pretty one, embroidered with love – but a serviceable utilitarian shroud-like thing which had been used many times, judging by the stains on it. I knew what Helen was thinking. She was wondering how many babies that blanket had covered, and whether they'd been allowed to remain with their mothers.

She meant to fight off sleep, but couldn't manage it.

I stood guard over the cot, but they came for her.

'Now just you put that baby down!' I demanded crossly, haranguing them as they walked down the corridor with it, but of course no one listened to me. Powerless, I was.

'And yet I thought?' Marcia interjects again.

'That I have ultimate power?' I shake my head, trying not to mind the interruption. 'It's not as easy as you think, you see. I'm more like the UN peacekeeping forces, who have to witness but stand aside.'

When Helen woke and saw the empty cot, she was devastated.

At night, sometimes she thought she could hear a baby crying and she'd walk the corridors in search of her daughter.

There was a wing of the house they kept barred from the patients.

Helen believed they kept Hetty there.

She would search and search throughout the night, always ending up in front of the heavy door they kept locked, banging her fists against the white frosted glass. But no one let her in.

Then one day she looked down onto the gravel drive, and saw a lady and gentleman leaving Topliffe Hall. The lady wore a black feathered hat. She carried a white bundle in her arms.

Helen slapped the glass and screamed.

'Dear, dear,' Mrs Foreman pronounced later. 'Just when we thought we were arriving at a cure.'

For years, Helen waited for a visit from her father.

'There has been some kind of mistake,' she told them, as she looked up from her sewing.

'There's no mistake, dear.'

'Has my father been yet? I'm waiting for a visit from him.'

The nurses shook their heads.

'She's cuckoo, that one.'

One of them leaned close towards her. 'Your father died forty years ago, dear.'

Helen looked at them, dazed. 'There must be some mistake,' she repeated. 'I shouldn't really be here.'

One of the new nurses laughed. She was youthful, didn't really want to work here. She wore make-up, even though it wasn't allowed. Helen hadn't noticed her before.

'It was Doctor Hughes, you see,' Helen said. 'He was the one. And my father trusted him. He needs to know.'

'Know what, dear?'

It came as no surprise, to me at least. It's an old, old story.

There were no mirrors at Topliffe Hall, but the young nurse took out a powder compact from the pocket of her uniform, and handed it to Helen.

'Seen yerself lately, have you?'

I thought that was rather cruel.

I watched Helen lift the small looking-glass to her face. She didn't recognize the woman staring back at her. She reached up a bent, bony finger to touch her grey hair. Then she handed back the powder compact.

'There must be some mistake,' she murmured.

When they made Topliffe Hall into luxury apartments for the elderly a few years back, many of the residents complained – as I said – of hearing a baby crying at night. Some assumed it was a relative visiting one of the other flats, but no one reported having an infant staying with them overnight. They searched and they searched, along corridors, down the service stairs, in the basement and attics, but there was never any sign of an abandoned baby. There were no children living there at all. Just retired couples. Well-off, good pensions, most of them.

They say Helen still walks the corridors at night, in search of Hetty. She bangs on the glass doors, but when the residents look, there's no one there.

'And what of Hetty? What became of her?' Marcia asks.

'Ah, now there's another story. But I think we'll save that one for another time.'

Dunblane 1996

'Are there occasions when you long to warn your victims?' Marcia asks, quite out of the blue.

'Well, I wouldn't really call them victims. I prefer the term human beings. Yes, there are many times when I would give anything to be able to warn them, but it's just not possible, I'm afraid. What will be, will be.'

'It is all fated then, in the stars?'

'Now there's a question. And I'm not sure I'm qualified to answer that.'

'Well if *you* can't, who can?'

'Good question.'

She looks at me, perplexed, and I can't say I blame her. It's so easy to evade the truth, avoid a confrontation.

'Don't expect too much of me, Marcia, you know?'

In truth, I begin to wonder if I am a bit of a disappointment to her. You see, one thing I have learnt over the years is that human beings like to believe that everything happens for a good reason, that we live in an ordered universe. But we don't. Embedded within that perfect construct is chaos. We share a flawed universe, you and I. Beautiful, wonderous, but essentially flawed.

It's quite terrifying to live in a random universe, where things just happen.

And if there is a reason, it's never a good one.

A quarter of a century ago, I was called to a place where I did not want to be. I would have given anything not to be there. I'd have given the world, sacrificed everything I owned.

But duty called.

And away I went.

Not very far, as it happens.

A small Scottish town with a cathedral that seems too vast for its humble setting, and a river running through the middle, dividing the town in half, a train-track dividing it in half again.

It was snowing.

And it kept on snowing.

A man arrived in a van, carrying legally-held weapons, licenced to him with the permission of the upper echelons of the police force, the Chief Constable of Police. In fact, he was known in the Freemasons for doing little odd jobs, homers, I think you call them, locksmith or joinery jobs on the cheap. It's handy, isn't it? To know someone who can fix your locks, your cupboards.

I think you might know what happened next, where he parked, what he did, who he killed, who he maimed. You might not know the intricate details, because who would want to know? But you can look them up. There was a lot of press coverage at the time.

You'll know all this.

But what you might not know are other things. The warnings. Oh, I did my best to warn those at the top, with what limited powers I had at my disposal. Police officers had three times sent memos stating, *revoke this man's gun licence. And if you cannot revoke it, then do not renew it next year*. Words to that effect. Words which fell on deaf ears. The memo arrived on the Chief Constable's desk, and he stamped it. NO FURTHER ACTION. Three times, for three years running. Despite warnings from police officers and others.

I laugh. Bitterly. And Marcia looks worried.

'So, you ask me, Marcia, if I ever try to warn my victims. Well, I'm up against it with you lot, as you can see.'

The gun lobbyists, the gun clubs, they liked their sport. They enjoyed it, got a lot of pleasure from the precision and skill required. I can understand that. We all like to develop a skill.

So there *were* warnings. Just not to the right people – the parents of the children who were killed, for instance, or who were injured.

No one said to them, did you know that anyone can carry a handgun that can kill at least seventeen people in under three minutes?

It's funny, you know, because three days before, he asked a police officer (retired), 'How long would it take for the C.I.D. to respond to a firearms incident in Dunblane?'

Eleven minutes, he was told.

No one said to him, 'but why are you asking?'

Eleven minutes.

Time enough to kill himself before the police had a chance to shoot him.

Time enough...

He had a plan. He'd rehearsed it, you see.

So, Marcia, everything does happen for a reason. It

wasn't an accident. It didn't just happen because these things do.

It happened because three memos warning officials were marked for NO FURTHER ACTION. It happened because no one wanted, at the time, to ban automatic handguns.

It happened because no one listened to the warnings. And those who were alarmed enough to issue warnings, recommendations, demanding action.

Where are they now?

Growing beards in the countryside. Quietly ostracised.

And those who did not listen?

Nicely retired on a fat pension.

No questions asked.

They conducted an inquiry, in hushed halls in Stirling with a gallery of public witnesses, and a long screed of a document was produced with its findings. But as everyone knows, the great thing about a public inquiry is that it shuts everyone up. Lays the ghosts. Absolves even while it condemns.

And something – we don't know what – was locked away in a file for a hundred years. Whatever is in that file cannot be released until another three quarters of a century have passed, by which time, Marcia, many of those alive today will be dust.

'But not you?' she asks.

'Not me. I will still be here, bearing witness. Much good may it do me.'

Marcia looks so uncomfortable, I almost take pity on her, but it's hard to know all of this, and keep silent.

You might not even know about the ripples that are

still felt a quarter of a century later. Ripples which go on and on.

Just like the snow that fell that day, and the next, and the days after it. It covered the snowdrops that had fearfully bloomed at the roots of old trees. It covered the moor above the town, and it lay thick on the graves of dead people who had already become a historical footnote and knew nothing of what transpired that day, because their lives were over.

Helicopters juddered in the sky, mapping the territory. Trauma shivered in the air. Flowers washed up in tidal waves of cellophane and plastic blooms.

And the trees on Holme Hill where the rooks sat bore witness to wave after wave of funerals, black hearses, tiny coffins, silent crowds not daring to speak, in case out of their mouths came a wail.

Anyway, *Yours Truly* had a hard job of it that day. I hovered over that little town, and to some extent I've never left it.

But after the snowdrops come the daffodils. And it does stop snowing. Eventually.

Even though it starts again, the next year. And the next. And the one after that.

'I remember that day,' Marcia says.

And just like everyone else, she tells me what she was doing that day, how she heard about it.

'D'you know, some things are too much, even for me, Marcia. I'm not invincible you know.'

'I think I can see that,' and she appears to be offering me sympathy.

Me!

'It wasn't my fault.'

'I know,' she says.
'I didn't want to be there.'

It took me a while to leave that town. There was a young woman I used to like to visit. Lived in a boxy grey house on the hill.

I knew she was struggling.

I'd sit on the end of the bed while she and her husband lay sleeping, waiting for her to wake up, which she did several times each night. Haunted. There were many like her.

Four o'clock in the morning and she'd wake suddenly, with a jerk. It wasn't the baby who woke her.

Hana would pull herself upright and glance at the cot. Without disturbing her husband, she'd leave the warmth of the bed, lean over the cot, and watch the gentle rise and fall of her daughter's rib cage, frail as a bird's wing.

Moonlight fell in bars across the room.

Hana was reassured by her daughter's breathing. She often woke like this, in a panic, as if she feared something terrible would happen. So far it hadn't – not to her, anyway. But Hana knew she must be on her guard, always. The future yawned, a dark chasm, waiting to swallow her whole; something to be feared, just in case it stole away the one thing she held most dear.

It was Life that taught her to feel this way. Life with a capital L. Bad things don't happen to ordinary people, who live in ordinary towns. Do they?

Her daughter was twelve weeks old, happy and

healthy. She cried a lot at night, but then most babies do. Hana didn't get much sleep, and often had to hold her daughter while she performed simple household tasks. Her arms sometimes ached with the effort.

Hana had no family nearby, and her husband was leaving for the States the next day, on professional business. For they were all professional people, competent, secure. Hana hadn't yet told anyone about her fears or her panic attacks. She just tried to manage them as best she could, and of course she sensed me, sitting there, on the end of the bed, staring.

She knew I was there. Hence, her vigilance. She could not afford to drop her guard, and the effort of that was exhausting.

It was the early hours of the morning when Alistair left. Hana was sound asleep as he bent to give her a perfunctory kiss, and then dragged his small suitcase from the cupboard. He'd be gone for one week. A week that stretched ahead of Hana with terrible bleakness.

At lunchtime a kind neighbour dropped by, to see how the baby was getting on. I sat in a corner of the living room and watched, as Hana made coffee and desultory conversation, dribs and drabs about this and that. She looked a little strained, odd, as if remote from everything.

Then Judith began to tell a story about a friend whose child had died of cot death several years ago.

Bad idea, I thought. If I could have silenced that woman, I would have done, but no one ever listens to me.

Hana listened while the neighbour spoke, fixing her terrified gaze upon her daughter.

'Yes,' Judith went on, 'she was ten weeks old when it happened. Of course they went on to have four others, all grown up now, and they rarely speak about Ruth, the little one they lost. But she was in a corner of the sitting room when it happened, surrounded by her family. Lying on the hearth rug, she was. She simply stopped breathing. It was very sad. Hard to believe it's twenty years ago now.'

Hana stared at the kind neighbour and forced a smile. 'I thought cot deaths mostly happened when the baby is left sleeping on its own?' she said out loud.

But the kind neighbour Judith shook her head with a satisfied air. 'She was in the corner of the living room when it happened, surrounded by her family.'

'Well, you take care then,' the neighbour called as she left.

Hana offered polite platitudes, closed the door behind her unwelcome guest. She and I were left alone with the poison of Judith's story, passed down like a piece of secondhand clothing no one wants. And now Hana was left with it. It lay in the corner of the room, discarded.

And there was I, *Yours Truly*, perched on the end of the sofa, wishing I could offer a crumb of comfort, advice even.

Hana didn't look in my direction, terrified to meet my gaze.

She switched on the TV and turned the sound down.

She had known me ever since the day I first arrived in town. She'd felt me, seen me, watched me standing at street corners, unable to leave.

Hana noticed nothing odd about herself at first.

She dressed her daughter Leah, took her out into the sunshine, collected three-year-old Joshua from nursery. She was very tired, and very drained, but that, surely, was normal?

When she returned to the house she noticed the silence as she opened the front door. Part of her wanted to run away. *Yours Truly* was waiting for her, of course, leaning in the kitchen doorway, a cup of tea in my hand. Silent witness in the corner of every room she entered. Helping myself to the cups and saucers, the kettle, the hand towels. I cleared up behind myself. I'm good that way.

She turned on the TV, as a way of filling the silence, and fed Leah. *Teletubbies* kept her son Joshua entertained for a whole fifteen minutes.

He had his usual bedtime. He liked his routine of story, bath and bed. Perhaps to make up for the furious energy that spurted through him the rest of the day.

The house grew silent again, and I watched as Hana would not allow herself the luxury of a break. She kept the baby beside her on the sofa, just in case *Yours Truly* slipped in to do a quick snatch without her noticing. Hana knew that the world around her children teemed with hidden dangers. Insidious, invisible, toxic forces.

I came and sat on the sofa beside her.

That's what happens when you suffer from depression, you see.

I slip into the seat beside you, as you try desperately hard to ignore my presence.

She distracted herself with a book, but was too tired to read.

It was ten o' clock at night when she noticed

something odd. A raspberry-coloured rash on the back of Leah's neck. Panic overwhelmed her. She had no one to ring and ask. How could she? They would think she was mad, weak, suspect in some way.

During her short journey as a mother, Hana had observed that other mothers appeared to relax; they coped with an apparently effortless ease and competence.

They wrote lists, they budgeted, they changed nappies, they whizzed about in people carriers; they never looked tired or frazzled. They never longed to sit on their own and daydream.

They never sat in the doctor's surgery on routine visits and ended up reading all the posters about incidents of choking and meningitis (all statistics helpfully provided). They never suspected the worst. They believed that every day the sun would rise on their perfect world and nothing bad would ever happen.

They were dismissive of mothers like Hana as nervous and weak. She was a social aberration, an embarrassment. Post-natal depression and an inability to cope was a working-class disease, everyone knew that. Like drugs, or alcohol addiction.

'Well, you just have to get on with it, don't you?' they told her.

It was too late to disturb anyone with phone calls and worries. She must simply sit it out until morning, ride the fear, until the fear went away.

At half past ten exactly (I happened to check the clock at this point) Hana realised she had been staring at her daughter's chest, without pause, just to make sure she took her next breath.

You see, the story of the cot death had left its mark. It wasn't Leah we needed to worry about here. It was the impact it had on the mother, for she could no longer trust that Leah's chest would rise and fall as it had risen and fallen for the past twelve weeks. The next breath depended on Hana, the mother. So she was forced to watch, diligently, never allowing her gaze to shift. For half an hour this state of paralysing fear persisted.

It was painful to witness.

Eventually, I tapped her on the arm, tried to bring her back to the moment. She met my gaze then, and I smiled. 'I'm not coming for you. Or your children. Not yet,' I reassured her.

'You're a woman,' she noted quietly. 'How could you?'

I shrugged, and told her what I will tell you. 'What did you expect? It's always the women who clean up the mess.'

She had another week of this to bear before Alistair would come home from the sunny U.S. of A.

She knew that something was wrong. It couldn't be normal to feel such fear. And certainly it's not normal to see *yours truly*, sitting in a corner of the living room, helping herself to the bowl of fruit left lying.

But what could Hana do?

This is what she did.

She waited until morning.

And in the morning her child was still breathing… one breath after the next.

In and out. In and out.

Hana, a woman who felt things, breathed with her…

Boy

'Schools are interesting places, of course, I tell her.

There was a street in Motherwell where a young girl was killed by a motorist, going above the speed limit. Just a few notches. But enough to kill.

No speed bumps or traffic-calming devices. It's not a middle-class area.

I used to watch how the other kids would react. One boy in particular.

He had to pass by the spot every day on his way to school. There were flowers in cellophane lying on the pavement, cards, balloons, a tide of plastic and paper, left there as mementos at the spot where she died.

He tried not to think about it as he hurried past. Hands in his pockets, collar up. He was late for school again. He was always late, every day. His mum wasn't really a morning person.

'I had another bad night again, son,' she coughed from her bedroom.

If she couldn't be bothered to get up on time, why should he? I couldn't blame him, in all honesty.

He put on a show of bravado at school, pretending he didn't care.

He was pulled up before he'd even got through the main entrance. I managed to push my way in through the swing doors after him, just before the glass whacked me in the face.

'You're late again.'

Mr Bagshawe, blocking his way like a big combine harvester, his glasses glinting.

I stood beside Boy, biting my lip, almost as if I was the one in trouble.

No point in arguing, the boy thought. What could he say? Yes, he was late. A fact was a fact.

'Where's your tie, boy?'

He didn't have a clue, but he knew better than to say.

'Where should you be, boy?'

At home. Or by the river, fishing. But again – he knew better than to reply.

Bigshot Bagshawe they called him.

'My name's not Boy.' I nudged him, but it was too late. Out it popped. The first bit of insolence. I rolled my eyes, waiting for the gallows moment.

'What did you just say to me?'

I watched Boy struggle for an answer. Was he supposed to reply, or stay silent? He wasn't really sure which would be the best option in the circumstances. I couldn't advise him, and anyway, no one was listening to me. They never do.

Bigshot Bagshawe was not pleased, that much was evident.

All in all, it wasn't a good start to the day. But then again, I could tell already that Boy was used to that.

Kicking a football about in the yard, having a quick smoke before class with his pals, he could deal with that. But it was when he passed inside those gates, walked those grey corridors, stared at the rows of desks. That was when the trouble began.

It'd been like that since the beginning. People

calling him stupid because he couldn't read, because the letters danced in front of his eyes, making no sense.

'Look it up in a dictionary, Boy,' Mrs White had yelled at him, when he couldn't spell a word like 'whent'.

He grinned at the rest of the class, knowing that was one way to save face. Make himself look funny, because they were all laughing at him anyway. Might as well use it to his advantage.

But what Mrs White didn't get was that he sometimes didn't know where to find the word in the dictionary, because he never knew exactly which letter it began with.

Calling him dyslexic didn't make it any easier. It was just one more label, but he knew what they really thought of him.

In English I watched him doodling on his class jotter. Nothing made any sense to him. It hurt his head and made his brain feel fuzzy, like it was full of broken glass.

Mrs Langford, his English teacher, let him sit at the back and daydream. As long as they left him alone, that was all he asked. He just didn't want the spotlight on him.

And he absolutely hated it when they sent Mrs Mare to sit with him. She had a face like a sad horse and treated him like a sick patient in a hospital. She was full of professional tolerance, and drew attention to the fact he had a 'problem'.

He wasn't stupid. He knew what to make of people, what they were thinking. He just couldn't spell. If he tried to read or write, the letters played tricks on him, turned themselves into secret code that couldn't be broken. Even if you picked up a hammer and smashed it against them. Still the code wouldn't break. It would just stare back at him. A brick wall, shutting him out. Hurting his head.

So he daydreamed instead.

He looked out of the window at the hills beyond Motherwell, empty spaces that marked the edges of town.

A memory came, and he held onto it as something precious.

One trip to an island, where the sea moved and the breezes blew and the air was full of light. Sitting on a log on the beach, sand between his toes, staring out at the water. Sitting in a boat, pulling mackerel from the sea, glinting rows of them. That was the only time life had ever made sense for this Boy.

Mrs Mare, the classroom assistant, wasn't available today, thank God. Sitting with some other poor kid in another classroom probably. So he was free to daydream.

I sat in the desk beside him, watched him. Mrs Langford, bless her, had no idea she had a new pupil in class that day. *Yours Truly*, trying to blend in.

All through English, he remembered that beach, the boat, the silver mackerel he caught from the sea. The fire they lit, a long time ago.

He drew it in the margins of his exercise book. He drew the boat, the fish, the sea, the beach, the log he sat on, and the fire. He was so busy doodling that he didn't hear the footsteps coming up behind him. I hissed at him, nudged him, but nothing worked. And then it was too late. She stood behind his desk, peering over his shoulder.

He looked up quickly, tried to cover the page with his arm.

Mrs Langford's eyes narrowed.

Oh dear, I thought. Here we go. Poor Boy is in for it again.

The rest of the class were sniggering. So he sniggered back, waiting for it all to start, to be accused of not following instructions, of being lazy and ignorant, to be sent outside to await his fate.

But to both his and my surprise, Mrs Langford didn't say anything. She passed on, inspecting the other desks.

When the bell went, the class filed out, throwing their jotters on the pile.

He was quick to head for the door, always keen to escape.

She called him back. He thought about bolting it down the corridor, but a couple of boys were blocking his way. Everyone was sniggering, laughing. They knew he'd be pulled up again. He always was, and they smirked at him in passing.

He laughed it off, tried to pretend he enjoyed the notoriety of always being in trouble with Bigshot and the other teachers, but he didn't fool me. I knew how he really felt.

Mrs Langford had pulled his jotter from the pile. She opened it, and pointed to the page he'd been scribbling on.

He slouched with his hands in his pockets, and I slouched next to him. I almost reached up to check my tie, until I realised I wasn't wearing one, and that no one could see me anyway.

Boy sighed, waiting for the inevitable.

I kicked him, as if we were partners in crime, like a couple of teenagers. He frowned, but that was all.

She pointed at his doodles across the page. And then she said something which made both our jaws drop.

'You're very good at art, did you know that, Liam?'

He stared at her. And so did I. For a start, she'd forgotten to call him Boy, like everyone else.

He was at a loss for words. *I* didn't even know his name was Liam.

She studied the boat, the log, the fish being pulled from the sea.

'You should keep drawing, Liam.'

The two of us stood there, dumbstruck.

'Make sure you do.'

'Yes, Miss.'

Then he left the classroom. I took one look at Mrs Langford then bolted out after him.

'Wait for me,' but he was already halfway down the corridor.

On the way home, at the end of a long difficult day, we passed the spot again. The spot where the young girl died. But there weren't any flowers this time. Nothing. No balloons. No tokens of remembrance and sorrow fluttering in the breeze. Just a bare sidewalk, with a couple of plastic bottles and an empty packet of crisps left lying.

I blinked.

Time-lapse? This happens sometimes, confusing both me and my clients.

A twelve-year-old girl appeared from between two parked cars, running.

'Hi Liam!' she called.

He nodded.

'Stop running,' a voice shouted after her. 'You should look first.'

I looked back at the row of houses she'd emerged from, caught a glimpse of a tired parent, before the door slammed shut again.

The girl ran on, pony-tail bobbing, as a car narrowly missed her.

Next time it would be different.

Liam stood still and watched her, perplexed. There was a frown on his face as if he wanted to warn her.

I patted him on the arm.

There was much more to this Boy than met the eye.

Dark Comedy

'I had the privilege of interviewing Sue Townsend once,' I say.

'The writer? What was that like?'

'Well, she told me a very sad story about her childhood, which she had never shared with anyone before.'

She was eight years old, sitting up in the tallest tree, high in the air where no one could see them. There was a boy either side of her, Gary and Stephen. 'I *think* those were their names,' she said. 'People come and go when you are eight years old. One minute you're the best of friends, bonded for life, the next, you can't remember what they look like, or who they began hanging out with instead. There was no rupture or schism. No one fell out. We just moved on. Maybe because we wanted to forget our communal sense of guilt.'

It was the summer.

It's always the summer when you're eight. Their homes were in a terrace of red brick narrow houses in Leicester, but nearby was the wood – the dangerous wood that had yet to become dangerous. Green leaves shivered in a bright cloud around these three, and they were elevated above it all. The streets and their crowded homes were far away and they were here, floating in an Enchanted Forest. There were portals everywhere and this tree was one of them, high above a forest, surrounded by a scrappy housing estate. It was freighted with innocence and secrets. Grimm-like, with a tiptoeing wolf, a girl in a red cloak, and maybe a gingerbread cottage at the end of a twisty lane, with lollipops for chimneys.

'I was scruffy, a bit dirty, and happy,' Sue told me. 'I was utterly myself. No one had yet told me I couldn't be. I played with the boys, I ran faster than any of them, and I never tired of running. I came home from school on my own and unlocked the back door, fed the dog, took the milk bottles from the doorstep – three white skittles – and put them in the fridge, waited for the others to come home. Ran out to play. In the winter under a lamp post like D. H. Lawrence; in the summer in the woods like the children in *The Magic Faraway Tree* and no one knew where I was. I was always late home for tea, I never wore a watch and I never knew the time. I didn't brush my hair and I screamed when my mother washed it once a fortnight so she had to warn the neighbours. I don't remember brushing my teeth. There wasn't time to be clean. There was only time to play.'

'I liked to be naughty,' Sue said, 'to do forbidden things like trespassing in our neighbour's yard to play on their go-cart while they were away, so that the woman on the other side came out and yelled at us, telling me I should know better. Or we'd pick berries from the posh boy's garden – mainly because he had a garden.'

She plotted to run away, drew a map from memory (inaccurate) and began squirrelling away secret food supplies in preparation for the journey. She got as far as one chocolate Club biscuit in the bottom of a brown leather shopping bag, then forgot all about it.

'Look,' she said to Gary or Stephen, opening the bag to show them what she'd saved so far. They peered in at the lonely Club biscuit at the bottom of the bag and nodded at the gravity of her purpose, impressed and a little frightened of her. And she really meant to do it. She really believed she would run away. But then something else came along and like all eight-year-olds, she couldn't remember what happened to the Club biscuit and the bag, only that she forgot about them.

So they sat high up in the tree that summer, swinging their legs, all plans to run away forgotten. And below them a girl they knew, Anna Louise, walked alone. They noted her, the way children do, in silence.

'She was older than us,' Sue told me. 'Twelve. Which in our eyes put her in the maternal category, old enough to mother the rest of us.'

What happened next was a scene in a silent movie that Sue never spoke about – ever.

A man appeared below them, dragged Anna Louise backwards, his hands at her throat. He dragged her like a doll, so that her feet scraped a twin channel in the leaves on the ground. He pinned her against a tree trunk and they watched, while he strangled her.

'We didn't try to stop him. We did nothing to save her while she struggled.'

Then the man left. He ran away. He didn't look up.

'He never saw us hanging there above him.'

I waited patiently for her to continue, as she wept with the grief she had never shared before. This was her deathbed confession, which she was sharing with *yours truly*, and at such times I need to be extra sensitive. It's important to wait, to listen. She sniffed, lifted her head, and went on.

'I remember we jumped down from the tree – Gary, Stephen and me – skipped over her body, and ran out of the woods.'

Sue could not remember if they told anyone.

The police came.

The girl was found.

It was a big deal in the papers for a while, in the Leicester Mercury, but no one remembers her name now.

Sue could not forgive herself.

'We did nothing to save her, or to stop him.'

They skipped over her limp white legs, like children in a fairy tale, but the magic had gone from that wood. There were no more portals, no more enchanted forests, no more magic faraway tree. The gingerbread cottage was best avoided.

It's easy to build up a new universe to replace the one you lost. You just avoid certain routes in case they trigger a memory, detonate a hidden land mine. You all do it. I watch you avoid the wormholes in your lives.

'I never spoke to Gary or Stephen again,' Sue said. 'It was the end of the summer for us. But I would like to ask them if they remember, if they feel guilty too.'

She stopped reading Enid Blyton that year. She stopped believing in fairies, magic wishing chairs and portals. She didn't know it then, when they sat in that tree, but she would one day grow up to write dark comedy.

Comedy is so close to tragedy, you see.

'I don't know where Gary and Stephen are now. I don't know if those were their real names,' she said.

She invented a diary for a teenage boy. You'll know his name. He was always struggling with the onset of a perpetual puberty and troubled by unattainable ambitions.

In all those pages, though, devoured by millions of readers and broadcast on national TV, Adrian Mole never once saw a girl murdered, or stepped over a dead body in a leafy wilderness. As Sue herself said, some things just don't make good comedy.

The Camping Trip

'Let me tell you about some of the good times,' I tell Marcia.

'Please,' she says.

'I make friends with you, before the end. I walk beside you, familiarize myself with your little foibles and idiosyncrasies, your likes and dislikes. And a lot of you are really good company, I have to say.

In getting to know some of you, I'm often afforded the perks of a little holiday, a camping trip maybe.'

'Like a busman's holiday?'

'Is that what they call it?'

'It's just a phrase, but I think I know what you mean.'

It had been Orla's idea to go wild camping for a few days. In Scotland you had to grab your moment. If no rain was forecast, then sleeping bags, tent, books, miniature stove and tea-making equipment were flung into the back of the car, and off they went.

And on this occasion, I went with them.

Sat in the back seat with the dog, although of course Ruth and her grown-up daughter had no idea I was there. The dog did, but I paid him no heed. He kept trying to lick my nose, but I batted him off.

I'd been living inside Ruth's head for quite some time now, as she worried herself sick about what the future held. Hospital visits, treatment denied.

I knew that it was twenty-five years since she'd first

moved to Scotland, but Ruth still couldn't get over the excitement of finding stunning mountains, lochs and forests on her doorstep. She remembered days of frustration in London, stuck in a traffic jam for hours before catching a glimpse of a field.

She was fifty-four this year and had recently gained a sense of her own mortality. This camping trip was a rare opportunity to spend some time alone with her daughter.

Dusk came, and with it, the noises of the night.

I was terribly excited to be with them. This camping trip was a rare treat indeed. So simple, yet so perfect, in the end.

Mother and daughter settled down inside the tent with much hilarity, the silence broken by the sound of zips being quickly drawn to keep out the flies.

Orla's two-man had a blackout lining and was midge-proof if kept closed, so they installed themselves and the dog inside its nylon womb, zipping up behind them, the loch still visible through the netted porthole. They had Indian cushions, pillows, an old quilt arranged on top of the sleeping mats, and battery-powered fairy lights strung from the zip hooks above them.

There wasn't room for me.

I sat outside on the rocks and looked at the stars.

'It's not exactly glamping, but it'll do,' I heard Ruth say to her daughter.

Orla lay reading her book by torchlight, the dog sleeping on her chest, while her mother rustled a bit inside her sleeping bag.

They could hear a tent flap knocking gently against the side of the tent, teased by the wind.

Out on the loch, the quiet island breathed, attached to the mainland by only a thin strip of sand. They had found the perfect wild spot, miles from anywhere.

Oh, the pleasure.

I could hear an owl in the trees on the bank opposite. Softly calling me. It knew I was there. Pause of five minutes, before it called again. It felt primitive. I'm no ecologist, Marcia, but that forest felt ancient.

Voices.

I sat up.

Ruth, inside the tent, could hear them cutting across the water.

Male voices, rising to a laddish yell, then lowering again to a faint murmur.

Orla lay still, but Ruth tensed, listening hard.

Where were they? How far away?

In the trees?

She sat bolt upright as the whooping drew nearer.

They didn't sound like they were on the roadside above the loch.

She reached out a hand, unzipped the tent opening, then peered out.

'They're in a boat,' she hissed.

I knew this already. I could see them, heading our way.

Orla rustled about inside her sleeping bag and came to peer out beside Ruth.

Faintly, in the shadows, the smudgy grey outline of a kayak came into view, two figures inside it, heading straight for the island. *Our* island.

We three women, I felt, had laid claim to this little territory and it would bear no intruders.

'Where are my car keys?'

'Why?'

'Dan always tells me – hold them in your fist with the points sticking out between the knuckles, then – BAM!'

'If they were going to attack us, they wouldn't be arriving in a kayak.'

I couldn't help imagining what it was like thousands of years ago, when the only people to be seen here arrived by boat, like this. Old memories. Beautiful ones, but I did not have the luxury of indulging such idle daydreams at this moment. All my faculties were required, dealing with the oncoming threat.

The kayakers fell quiet, and as Ruth watched, the nose of the raft appeared to be heading directly for our own tree-lined shore.

Then, at the last minute, it swerved off to the left, rounding the tip of their island, and she could see the side of the kayak, still a soft grey outline in the dusk.

The kayaker in front whistled loudly to get their attention, before it finally disappeared from view.

Ruth lay down again beside her daughter, on full alert. What if they beached on the other side of the island, out of view, and decided to come investigating?

The tent flap rustled against the nylon, the wind breathed through the heather, and the water murmured over the stones.

I sat outside the tent on my rock. Kept watch. I liked these two women. I wanted to guard them.

But the inevitable happened. We all fell asleep.

I had no idea how long I had been dozing when the shouts echoed across the water again, from *behind* the island this time.

Orla slept on, unconcerned, but Ruth fidgeted. I could hear her inside the tent. She twisted to one side so she could hear properly.

She lay her ear on the ground to listen for any faint footfall on the stones outside.

Within minutes she was asleep.

The island around her continued to stir, but she didn't hear it.

I kept awake this time.

On guard.

Dawn brought relief.

As soon as Ruth opened her eyes she was amazed she had slept at all.

She swung their towels onto a high branch, laughed off her fears of the night before while they cooked breakfast and boiled the kettle for tea.

I hovered nearby, enjoying the camaraderie. No one offered me tea, but I'm a woman of fortitude. I can wait.

They lit another small fire: Ruth read her book while Orla curled inside the tent with the dog.

Then her daughter's head emerged.

'Time for the bathroom.'

'I think you'll find it's over in that direction,' and Ruth waved a hand vaguely towards the vegetation in the centre of the island.

She watched her daughter wander off, and gazed out across the loch.

I sat with Ruth for a while, saying nothing.

Did she see me?

She didn't once look in my direction.

Sandy footsteps broke the silence.

'We've got company,' Orla said.

'What?'

'Another tent on the far side of the island. They must have pitched there late last night.'

'Really?'

Ruth trotted off to check for herself, and I followed, just in case. The middle of the island was not as pleasant as the shore, with its clean beach of fine large stones and the waves lapping against the rocks. Clouds of midges lifted into the air as she brushed through the coarse blooming heather.

There. A small green canvas tent, blending so well with the trees, she hardly saw it. It was zipped tightly shut, as if its occupants were still sleeping.

She frowned.

So much for island wilderness, but they didn't have to come across one another. They could respect one another's privacy. The island was just big enough for that.

She climbed the next rise and scrambled down again towards the part of the island which stuck out into the centre of the loch – the bit she had yet to explore – then stopped dead.

'Hello!'

The voice first, startling her.

A short, bearded figure standing on the edge of the stones with his hands in his pockets. His hair was cut short, his beard was ginger, and he had the unmistakeable look of a Glaswegian about him: stumpy, with a comical twisted look in his eye. A bit mad-looking.

He acknowledged me with a nod, which was a bit disconcerting.

'Oh, I didn't realise there was anyone else on the island,' Ruth said.

He nodded matter-of-factly.

'Bit windier today!'

'Mm? Oh yes,' she said. 'It is a bit.'

'Been here long?' he asked.

'Er – we arrived yesterday. My daughter and I, we're doing a road trip.'

'Smashing.'

'Yes, it is.'

'Lovely bit of the world this.'

She nodded her agreement vigorously.

'Well, I'll let you get on then,' he added, and turned back to face the shore with his hands in the pockets of his shorts, staring out at the loch as if he had some important business to attend to.

'Strange,' Ruth murmured, as she stumbled away over the rocks.

I stayed behind.

Could he see me?

But he kept his back to me, so I stumbled off after Ruth.

It was impossible to do a dignified walk here, you had to concentrate on your footing or you'd be over in seconds, twisting an ankle.

I could hear the cogs ticking over in Ruth's mind.

What was he doing? she wondered. He wasn't

fishing or anything. He looked as if he was just staring, which of course people do all the time, but not with such an air of 'business' about it.

'Well, I think I've met our new arrival,' she told Orla as she skilfully wove her way around the guy ropes. 'Short bearded chap. Quite nice, actually. Not a threat at all. Although...'

There was always reason to doubt and be wary.

When they found the skull on the island and the pile of bones beneath a small cairn, things changed. Ruth wanted to leave immediately and contact the police, but of course their mobile phones were dead.

The cairn of stones sat on the beach, a short distance from their campsite. Orla began borrowing a few of the stones to add to their own campfire beside their tent, because the wind had picked up and the fire needed some form of shelter.

She lifted the boulders one by one, like round white loaves clicking together, and carried them across to their own campfire.

Ruth, watching, joined in.

But it was what lay beneath the stones that startled them. A clean white bone.

'A sheep?' Orla suggested.

Ruth glanced around.

'There ain't no sheep that I can see,' she said, using the jocular tone she adopted in a crisis.

Then the skull emerged. Orla had picked it up, mistaking it for one of the loaf-sized boulders. It grinned at her, Hamlet-like.

She dropped it on the shore and it clunked a little.

They both stood staring at it.

Before either of them could begin to panic or entertain dark thoughts of stumbling upon a murder victim the newcomer from around the other side of the island sauntered up, hands still in pockets.

I could tell Ruth didn't know whether to be alarmed or relieved to see him.

Company. Someone to share the news with.

'What have you found there then?' he asked, kicking the stones a little with his bulky sandal.

Ruth noticed his toes. He was flat-footed, but there was instant humour in the way he moved or stood.

Mother and daughter stood back to let the evidence speak for itself.

'I don't really know what we're supposed to do in an event like this,' she said. 'What do you suggest?'

The newcomer bent down and studied the skull.

'I don't think there's any forensic team in the whole of Scotland who'd solve this one. Whatever happened to that chap there is ancient history. We'll never know.'

'How can you tell?' Ruth asked, and Orla narrowed her eyes to study the man.

'I'm an archaeologist, sort of. I can tell.'

'Professional or amateur?' I wanted to ask, but I was too polite to put it out there. Besides, I wasn't sure he could see me. He was still blanking me, despite the earlier nod.

He certainly looked like an archaeologist, with his beard and his sandals, although his stocky humorous posture spoke of something less academic, more down-to-earth.

'See that?' He picked the skull up and pointed at

fissures and cracks in the side of it. Not a single tooth was left in its head. 'That's no modern murder victim.'

'Anyway,' Ruth laughed. 'Who's to say they were murdered? They might have asked to be buried here, far away from the madding crowd. I know I would.'

Orla glanced at her mother and frowned.

'People often have a DIY funeral now. Cut out the middleman,' she went on.

The Glaswegian glanced at her, a twinkle in his eye. I could tell he identified with her dark humour. It was nice to see that. I like people to make connections.

'Well, I think in those days they had no choice but to opt for a DIY burial. It wouldn't have been a Co-op funeral, let's put it that way, plate of sausage rolls thrown in for the guests.'

Orla stared at them both.

'I wouldn't worry about it,' he added. 'He's not!'

'We can't just leave it here,' Orla said.

'Well, what are we going to do with it?' Ruth suggested. 'Bag it up with the rest of our things and pile it into the back of the car?'

'No, of course not. But we'll need to let someone know.'

'Makes you think, doesn't it?' the newcomer said.

'I'm sorry?' Ruth asked.

'Makes you think… about who lived here. In the past. What it was like for them. What they found. How they lived.'

'Yes, it does.'

He sighed with contentment.

'That was my profession, you see. That's what I

lived by. But I wouldn't let it curtail the rest of your camping trip.'

Orla and Ruth glanced uneasily back at their own tent under the trees.

'Well, I suppose we'd better get on with making our fire then,' Ruth said. 'Orla is on stove duty. She's a better cook than me.'

'Nice.'

He watched them and smiled.

'Oh, I haven't asked your name,' Ruth added. 'I'm Ruth and this is my daughter, Orla.'

'Barry,' he said, grinning, and leaned forward to shake hands with them.

It all seemed very formal, with the bones and bleached skull still lying in a tumble between them. It was strange to watch them. I felt part of this little gathering by now.

'I think I'll leave this for now,' Orla said, 'and get stones from elsewhere for the fire.'

'I would!' Barry agreed.

So they left the cairn of stones, half-disturbed, with the discovery just beneath it, replacing a few of the boulders for form's sake, so that the bones were hidden from view again.

It was only afterwards that Ruth wondered why Barry had used the past tense when referring to his 'profession.' Retired maybe? He didn't look old enough.

I watched the grey beauty of another dusk softly approach across the water, leaving the loch full of shimmering light.

My companions had already eaten and washed their few pots. They'd shared a saucepan of curry together and ripped naan bread to mop up the juices. They sat either side of the fire for an hour, reading their books, until Orla retreated to the tent, taking the dog with her.

'I'll join you in a while,' Ruth said, listening to the rustle of nylon and the zipping of tent fastenings as Orla made herself comfortable.

Grey smoke trailed on the air. Ruth stretched out her feet and gazed across the water, nursing a plastic cup of red wine.

After a while she heard his footsteps on the pebbles. She nodded.

'Lovely evening.'

'Exquisite.'

'May I?'

'Of course,' and she gestured at the other stool, where he sat like a garden gnome, leaning close to the flames.

'Such a peaceful place this,' Barry offered.

'Have you been here before?'

'This is my first time, but I feel as if I've been here forever.'

She glanced at him, then her thoughts drifted back to the cairn of stones, and their gruesome discovery, although in truth it was not so gruesome after all. It was just nature. Bones and flesh returning to the earth.

'It makes you think about your own mortality,' Ruth said.

'You too?'

She thought for a moment, wondering how much

she should divulge, then decided that she might just as well tell a stranger as anyone. It was safer somehow.

'I have breast cancer.'

There was a small shocked silence. I already knew this, of course.

'I don't know how long I have left,' she added.

Barry took stock, and glanced towards the tent.

'Does she know?'

'My daughter? Not yet. I haven't told her. I will. Eventually. When the time is right. In the meantime there is this. And I mean to enjoy it.'

Barry gave another huge sigh of regret as he looked out across the water.

'Don't leave it too long,' he said. 'Just saying!'

She was surprised at how easy it was to confide in this stranger, and what a weight fell from her shoulders.

'In the end,' Barry said, 'none of us know when we're going to die. We don't know the hour or the place.'

'That's true.'

'We're all in the same boat. Or... to use a different euphemism, on the same island!'

Another small silence fell, while the waves whispered against the shore.

'Do you ever think about what comes afterwards?' Ruth asked.

'Afterwards?'

'After death,' she explained.

Barry shook his head.

'Nope! At least, I didn't used to. Before.'

'Before what?'

He shrugged. 'Before I came here.'

Ruth frowned.

'I don't understand. You've only just got here, haven't you?'

'In a manner of speaking.'

The conversation was beginning to go in circles.

Still, she liked Barry's company, I could tell. He was reassuring. She didn't know why.

'I wouldn't worry about any of it,' he said.

She laughed. 'That seems to be your usual policy. But in this case, we're talking about incurable cancer.'

He nodded. 'I know. But just remember,' he glanced around at the shimmering loch, the forested hillsides, and the faint glow of the tent where Orla was reading by torchlight, 'there is always this.'

Ruth gazed about her.

Barry was right. Ruth and her daughter were making memories, moments in time.

'Well,' he rose after a bit and said, 'It was nice to meet you, Ruth.'

He made eye contact, nodded and smiled, then walked away across the beach.

Ruth watched him go, frowning.

She remained by the fire until the light dimmed and then crawled inside the tent to join her daughter and the dog, where she snuggled up happily inside her own sleeping bag.

The night was quiet and she slept more soundly than she had done in months, her daughter sleeping beside her, their breath equally matched, the dog's warm body heavy against their hips.

I sat guard all night, but it was a pleasure. I watched

that moon rise and I watched the northern sky which never grows dark.

Orla nursed the gas flame of the tiny stove, while a stiff breeze blew between the trees. Ruth sheltered inside the tent. The constant play of the wind was tiring after a while and she looked forward to her morning cup of tea with a rare appetite.

It pained her to think of her children being left alone without her, but this was a cul-de-sac of thought she did not travel often. She could not afford to. Life was a cycle and she was part of it, and so were they, and life in its brevity was beautiful which she must never allow herself to forget.

She didn't want to suffer. She didn't want to be in pain.

She wanted to choose the moment when the time was right.

She would know it, when it arrived.

Another dawn, and the first cuppa of the day, to be followed by a dozen others. Her hours were punctuated by this ritual, one pot leading to another. It was perhaps the only certainty in her life. Earl Grey. Lapsang. Fine Assam. Ceylon. I almost envied her.

If she was listening to a radio play in the car and someone mentioned tea, and she heard the tinkle of a china cup against a saucer, she would hunger for one herself. She would get home and put the kettle on. Or if she was watching television, and someone poured from a pot, she had to get up and perform the ritual herself. A small obsession, but hardly an unhealthy one – which was partly why it was so unfair.

But again, she stopped herself.

No mileage in that route.

Bitterness didn't pay, it only led to more bitterness.

'Tea's ready!'

Orla's voice.

'Ah – just what the doctor ordered.'

'Now, I'm sorting through our supplies and I think we have four pot noodles left and a packet of bruschetta. From Lidl.'

'I don't care where it's from, as long as it's edible.'

Orla came to sit beside her mother and they sipped their tea in the tent entrance, as the breeze battered the nylon.

'I suppose we could always hunt for game and eat that,' Ruth suggested. 'It's not like we're starving.'

'Or… we could go and get a bag of chips? Except we're miles from any shop.'

'That's as it should be. I wanted the wilderness experience. And we've got it.'

'Apart from Barry,' Orla said.

'Apart from Barry. Actually, he's rather nice, you know.'

'You said that yesterday.'

'I might wander along after breakfast and see how he's getting on.'

Orla sipped her tea quietly.

The dog followed hopefully as Ruth strolled into the centre of the island, underneath the few trees. It took her precisely one minute. Beneath her lay the bay where Barry's green tent had appeared. She frowned, and it took her a moment or two to register what she was seeing. The spot where the tent had been was completely empty.

No tent.

Barry must have left early this morning, without saying goodbye.

A surge of disappointment hit her out of all proportion to the event.

He was the only person she had confided in, shared the burden of her dreadful news with.

A stranger.

And he took her burden, her news, and travelled away with it.

'He's gone.'

'What?'

'Barry! His tent's not there anymore.'

'Oh.'

'He must have left early this morning, before we were up.'

'That's a shame.'

Ruth sat quietly on the camp stool, watching the waves dash against the shoreline. All around her the world was wind and movement. The dog was tired of it, and wanted the inside of the tent.

'D'you think it's too cold for a swim?' Orla asked.

Ruth shrugged. 'Depends how brave we are.'

But all at once she wanted to feel the sting of cold water against her skin, the peaty-brown earthiness of it, even if it carried germs and bacteria and all the detritus and decay of wildlife.

Go for it, I whispered, but she didn't hear me of course. Or did she?

'Come on, let's give it a go,' she added. 'I'm game if you are.'

They changed into their swimming costumes and marched briskly down to the sandy part of the shore which joined their little island to the mainland.

Leaving towels and hoodies on a large stone, they stepped into the water and it curled around their knees and thighs until all sensation stopped, and then in they plunged, Orla first, then Ruth. Orla swam in easy luxurious strokes, wide and smooth, while Ruth floundered jerkily with the cold of it. But it felt good.

She felt alive.

She took time to look about her as she swam, at the forested hillsides, the olive-green shore, the stones, the sand, the sky with its scudding clouds.

I am outside and I am swimming in a loch, she was telling herself. And I didn't blame her. I shared her joy.

She was thinking, what would her twenty-four-year-old self have said to this, when she lived in Greenwich in a damp basement flat?

She would have envied me, and longed to do the same.

I have had fifty-four years, she thought, and it is enough. Enough to understand the beauty of life and be amazed by it.

And yet, it is not enough.

You all want more.

She was sorry that Barry had left. She hadn't liked the intrusion at first, but now they were alone again, she missed the idea of company, I could tell.

They ran back to their campsite with towels wrapped around them.

'Wait for me,' I called, but no one did.

Having changed quickly into warmer clothes, they felt cosy, clean and safe.

I envied them so much it caused an ache.

'It's warmed me up,' Ruth said. 'You?'

'Me too!' Orla replied.

'So, what do you think?' Ruth asked. 'One more night before we move on?'

'I think so,' Orla agreed.

'I'll just take a little walk.'

The dog followed, sniffing, as she negotiated the rocks and boulders along the beach, towards the side of the island which stuck out into the middle of the loch.

I followed too.

Just in case.

The dog was getting used to me by now, and paid me no attention. I was an accepted part of his pack.

When she heard his voice again she nearly jumped out of her skin.

'Hello!'

'You? Still here?' Ruth cried.

'Yep. Still here.'

'But I thought you left?'

'Why?'

'Your tent's gone.'

Barry laughed, a twinkle in his eye.

'Not my tent.'

'Then who…?'

He shrugged. 'Don't know. Never met them.'

Then he sighed again and looked out across the water with his hands in his pockets, in exactly the same posture as when she met him.

She frowned, and looked about her.

'But I don't understand.'

Barry didn't help to enlighten her. He was too busy studying the far bank of the loch and the pull of the current in the middle of the water.

'Where's your tent then?'

'My tent?' he repeated, hands still in the pockets of his scruffy shorts.

'Yes, yours.'

'I don't know, somewhere over there,' and he gestured vaguely toward the trees in the centre of the island.

'But there isn't one,' Ruth said.

His shoulders sagged. 'No, there wouldn't be.'

She stared at him, frowning.

'They probably took it away.'

'Took it away? What do you mean?'

'Mum…' We all heard her daughter's voice calling from the shore and turned to see Orla stumbling happily towards her over the stones.

'Over here!' Ruth called, waving.

When she turned back to speak to Barry, I knew what she would find. The space he had once filled was empty. He had gone.

'Shall we make another fire?' Orla cried, coming closer. 'What do you think?'

I watched Ruth hesitate for a moment.

'I think another fire would be perfect.'

We all sat together, by the flames. Ruth sat with Orla, Orla sat with the dog, and I sat between them all.

Although only the dog could see me.

And it was the happiest I have ever been.

The Parsonage

Like anyone else, I have my good times and my bad times. The good times, I have to admit, are few and far between.

'Tell me another of the good times,' Marcia says, and I oblige.

'It's so easy to slip into the mode of Curator of the Festival.'

'What festival?' she asks.

'The Bronte-Fest,' I reply. 'Those gifted women in their confining dresses, who strode across the moors in the rain.'

'Ah, I think I see where you're going,' and Marcia exhales a sigh of pure contentment.

I crammed myself onto the coach with everyone else. I don't know why. I just wanted to see what you'd make of it all since I'd last visited those draughty rooms with their high ceilings and icy-cold flags on the floors. I wanted to see it all through your 'modern' eyes.

So I caught the coach, squeezed into an empty seat opposite a couple from Barnsley, their rucksacks stuffed into the overhead rack. They were a bit dull, but I just stared out the window. It was then I discovered, to my intense discomfort and inconvenience, that I suffer from travel sickness.

I was facing the wrong way. Fields and moors and grim northern towns, whose hope had long fled, flew by, and I started to feel dizzy and nauseous.

Of course, as anyone who suffers from travel sickness will know, it is fatal if one of the other passengers decides to eat a banana.

Waves of nausea washed over me and as I retched into a hankie, I began to regret my down-to-earth policy of blending in with the people. I could have arrived by carriage if I'd wanted to, or on the back of a gleaming charcoal-black stallion. Something glamorous and romantic. But no, I chose the cheap 'away-day' by public transport.

They disgorged us in Haworth, for which I was so grateful. To breathe in great lungfuls of the fresh air, and to slip away from the couple from Barnsley, who, I could tell, were not really great readers. They were only there for the tea shops.

Who would have thought it? The Grim Reader can be a literary snob.

'That fits,' Marcia smiles, and I glimmer at her.

The cobbled street was sunlit and busy, and nothing like I remembered it when I came upon that family of geniuses so long ago. Frilly tea shops, gimmicky nonsense spilled out onto the cobbled incline, a steep hill leading up to the Parsonage.

Crowds brushed past me, unthinking. We were all on pilgrimage, to find the crock of gold.

There was a crush to get inside the house, so I lingered outside among the gravestones, thinking, remembering.

A massive snaking queue to buy tickets for the museum, with its glass cases full of precious exhibits, all tastefully procured. Charlotte's tiny shoe, a pair of pattens belonging to Aunt Branwell, a miniscule pair of lenses through which Charlotte once viewed the world; notebooks, pens, the bare kitchen where Emily ruled. The bed where Branwell died. The polished dining table around which they marched of an evening, with the wind howling, reciting their ideas to each other. The nursery wall, where childish drawings can still be seen, scribbled onto the plaster. A white handkerchief of Anne's with a blood-red rose still blooming on its snowy field, unfading, evidence of the beginning of the end.

I'm quite taken by it all myself.

Haworth Parsonage has made a cottage industry out of Death. They have out-deathed me. And who can blame them, for the legend is true. I saw it with my own eyes. I was there, reluctantly taking the hand of each, leading them away from their family fireside.

Months after *Wuthering Heights* and *Jane Eyre* were completed, three of them lay beneath the sod, their voices no more than echoes in the Parsonage, while Charlotte remained to linger for a few more years alone, mourning the loss of her siblings.

I remember it without the curators and the glass cases, without the museum and the tea shops. I remember a house full of laughter, a house full of pain, a house full of children who were completely normal and original, in that they lost loved ones, laughed and cried, disappeared into fantasy. Home-schooled to perfection, except when they were sent away.

They cooked each other in a perfect stew of creative juices, fed one another's hunger, slaked one another's thirst. They did what all children who suffer a loss do. They made up stories, invented characters, built up a land of infinite possibilities in the normal way of all children. They drew pictures to illustrate their fantasy world, a place called Glass Town, with a whole cast of colourful characters who bore ominous names and might have stepped off the stage of an ancient Greek tragedy.

I loved those children. They lost two older sisters and a mother, and the survivors – Branwell, Charlotte, Emily and Anne – soldiered on as survivors do, building up a story they told themselves. It all began, in fact, with a present of tin soldiers which their father gave them, and from there, their imaginations took flight. We call it world-building. All healthy children engage in this pursuit at some point, if lucky, if encouraged. Some more than others.

You give them a little figure and they start pretending, putting on voices, imagining a life. Admittedly, it doesn't always lead to several classic masterpieces, but... hey ho.

Here at Haworth we were in luck.

So yes, I'd had my good times and my bad times at the Parsonage, but now I wanted to be a tourist, like the rest. A day off, taking in the sights, a little nostalgic trip down Memory Lane.

I sat on a gravestone, spread out my picnic – a ham roll grabbed from a motorway café on the way up – sipped a take-away coffee – and remembered.

How bare this place was, how grim, how cold inside those echoing rooms. How full the graveyard, how fearful the sights, how wild the wind.

Emily. She was the one who loved it all.

A cough disturbed me from behind, and I looked

up, and there she was. In fancy dress, like one of the curators themselves, hair coiled back, haughty glance, reserved.

I feasted my eyes on her in surprise.

And then she said something that completely threw me.

'You're in my seat!'

'I'm sorry?'

'I said... you're in my seat. I always sit here.'

I looked down at the gravestone I'd chosen as my picnic spot: nice solid table, half in sun, half in shade.

I got up clumsily, smiling politely. I knew who she was alright.

'Sorry, I had no idea.'

She nodded, and sat, her back to the Parsonage, and waited for me to speak.

I was dumbstruck. I didn't know what to say.

'I... I've always been a fan,' I managed, which seemed completely absurd, and she rightly ignored it.

The longest time passed, awkward as hell, before she said, 'I didn't expect to see you here.'

'You know who I am then?'

She snorted in disdain, as if this didn't require an answer, and kept looking forward.

'Is it always this busy?'

She shrugged and didn't answer, but I could tell she had her eye on my ham sandwich, so I offered her a bit. She declined, because, what else could she do?

'I thought you might be at peace, somehow, after all this time?' I offered.

'I am,' she said. 'This is where I like to be.'

A flutter of tourists drifted towards the door of the

church below us. We observed them in a detached, disinterested manner.

'How did you get here, by the way?'

'Funny you should ask that,' I said. 'The coach companies offer a cheap away-day ticket.'

She raised her eyebrows.

'I sat opposite a couple from Barnsley. Fans of yours, I imagine.'

Then she stood up without warning, and moved quickly towards the path up to the moor.

I followed, of course. How could I not?

'I just didn't expect to see you here,' I kept saying, stumbling after her, tripping on the big broken cobbles.

She had no trouble at all striding over that broken earth, glided almost, her strides long and confident.

She was, I understood perfectly, exactly where she wanted to be, and we walked together up onto that high moor, as the summer breeze blew through the grasses, and I knew she was privileging me with a rare treat.

It was a long walk, and to be honest, I needed it after the cramped bus journey with the banana disaster. I needed the fresh air, the high blowing wind, bearing the tang of peat and amber rust.

Sheep grazed, nibbling the moor, and ran when we approached, bleating for their lives, away from our ghostly duo.

We stopped in a gully, a dip in the moor, where water ran over the rocks, and a large stone formed the seat of a throne.

'I used to sit here,' she said.

'I know.'

I remembered her enthroned here, surrounded by moorland, her fingers exploring the stone beneath. If it rained, she got wet, when the wind blew, it dried her. When the sun shone, she raised her head, watched sheep-clouds sail past the horizon. If it snowed, she headed for home, knowing she could be lost like Lockwood.

We paused here a moment, then headed on, and as Emily strode ahead, I knew she was exactly where she wanted to be. She would walk this way forever.

Grasses parted, the path snaked higher, peaty waters trickled into downward slopes, a signpost marked the crossing of pathways where Nelly Dean might once have stood and watched Hareton throw stones at her.

Higher still and we reached the ruins. Top Withens, with its gable end and its single tree, bent and twisted by the wind. Empty doorsills and broken hearthstones, glimpses through windowless walls to the outside, to a place where outside was in and inside was out.

Emily stood still on an elevation above it all, and raised her profile. I watched her, knowing that this was what the tourists below would really like to see.

Here was Emily's perfect embodiment, her most sublime discovery: here was her leading character.

The power of the moor, with its windswept heights, its empty stage set for drama, its eternal backdrop of tragedy, where little human lives stay small forever.

She had found her main character, here, in the setting itself.

The moor was both heroine and hero of her classic story. She endowed it with life, performed the miracle of alchemy.

'You know, I really get why you love it here,' I said.

'Why I won't leave it?'

'Yes, I do.'

A feather had caught on her dress, soft as a snowflake. She breathed in, untouchable, while around her the dry air swirled.

It was her air, scented with the honeyed kick of heather and harebells, the musk of sheep leavings, and an almost invisible undertone of old mill workings, carried far from the grimy towns.

Later, I caught a lift back to the station with a family from Leeds, couldn't quite face a repeat of the coach journey.

Crammed in the back with the children, I gazed out the window as we passed the moor to our left. Way, way beyond the rolling fields and farmland, the open heath and moor, I saw those hills, and rightly identified them as the spot where she had led me to the ruins of Top Withens. And I thought I saw her there, a tiny dark figure, black against the bright air, against the brown earth. So far, and so high, and so untouchable.

I give a small laugh as I look at Marcia.

'There was no persuading her to leave. There she will remain. It's where she belongs.'

'So you didn't really get a chance to do the gift shop, then?' Marcia says.

I smile at her levity.

'No, Marcia. I didn't need to. I'd seen it all before.'

Lady Jane Grey:
12 February 1554

I am a collector of stories. I gather them together like a bundle of flowers, and press them between the leaves of my heart, until they are desiccated and dry, preserved for all time inside my own Memory Box. No one else has access to this Memory Box.

'Except me,' Marcia cuts in.

'Well, yes, of course. Except you. But you're not always here.'

'That's true.'

With the tea cooling between us, Marcia says she fancies another historical footnote. Something juicy. She suggests a famous name she has heard of, at random.

'Lady Jane Grey.'

Her wish is my command.

'The Tower of London must have been a grim place in those days?' Marcia suggests.

I hear the walls drip, muffled cries creating a distant echo.

'It was certainly cold. Jane had no fire in her cell.'

'Lady Jane Grey?'

I nod.

She was a child, caught up in the power games played by men – her ambitious father, for one, who married her off to the seventeen-year-old son of Northumberland in a bid to secure the throne for her.

She and the boy were victims in the whole charade. The Catholics prevailed and she was famously Queen for nine days only. After that, the two young things, after a long spell in the Tower, grew surprisingly fond of one another but were executed, one by one. Grist to the mill. Chaff in the wind. Innocents in the way of history.

She was a bright girl. Very intelligent. Lovely, in fact.

A wind blew through the rooms of the Tower at all times. It was a terrifying prospect, to be rowed under Traitor's Gate, knowing you would not be making the return journey. The water of the Thames was inky-black, sombre, flickering from the flaring torches that lit the prow of the boat.

Jane didn't fear for her life, at first. Everyone assured her the new Queen, the Catholic Mary, would take pity on her for being an innocent victim in all of this. Mary Tudor had had her own fair share of being at the mercy of ambitious men, fathers who cared little for their daughters. She was the daughter of Henry VIII, after all.

Jane's room was small, but well-lit. She had access to books. There was straw on the floor, to absorb the damp of the cobbles. Her window gave onto the courtyard beneath. She could see the Beauchamp Tower, where her young husband was imprisoned, and beyond that, Tower Hill. She was there from November 1553, when they first arrested she and Guildford Dudley. He was an innocent boy too, teenagers forced to marry as a political manoeuvre to secure power for their families.

Jane hadn't been inclined to marry so young, but

now that their fate was joined, the pair began to write to each other from their mutual confinement, seeking a little comfort, someone to share the burden with. He became a friend and confidante. They became very close. It's perhaps ironic that she fell in love with him, after all, and could have enjoyed a long and happy marriage, given a different set of circumstances.

After a few months of writing to each other, she sat at the window and watched as they led him from the Beauchamp Tower to his death on Tower Hill. He was seventeen years of age.

A woman called Elizabeth Tilney was with Jane. She had been her companion and helped to rear her throughout her youth.

'Queen Mary will take pity on you, Madame,' she reassured the girl, and comforted her when she cried.

I watched from my corner of the cell, invisible as ever, a woman out of time like all the rest. And neither Lady Jane Grey nor her lady's maid, Elizabeth Tilney, saw me. They were used to dealing in death in those days, muttering prayers and incantations to a God who never seemed to listen.

'Poor Dudley,' I heard her whisper, turning aside from her window which gave onto the place of execution.

I tried to remain discreet, as unobtrusive as possible. Perhaps her ladies were right, and the child would be spared. But this did not take into account the determination of Jane's father to cause mischief. When he was caught in rebellion a second time, Jane's fate was sealed.

For myself, I knew I could do nothing but lead her

to a premature death and kneel with her beside the executioner's block. It would happen. And I would need to be there, at the party. I did not want to, but as I have been at pains to explain, I have no choice in the matter. Destiny chose me. And Destiny chose Jane.

I watched her in her small bare room. She tried to read. She was cold, and I wondered why they didn't put her in a room with a fireplace.

I studied her slender neck. It looked so delicate, so fine. Like china or porcelain. One swipe would be sufficient. But of course women are not made of porcelain. They are blood and bone. Lots of it, pouring copiously from a severed neck. A crimson dash splashing onto the straw and cobbles.

They did not spare her, of course.

She was a child, but they were still prepared to take off her head in the name of politics and ambition. Power and greed.

A freezing wind blew as they led her out to the courtyard below the White Tower, and up the steps of the wooden scaffold.

It was bitterly cold, February, with fragments of snow floating in the air. The blade looked polished, glinting in the cruel light.

Mistress Allan and Elizabeth Tilney helped her.

She wore a black gown and was carrying an open prayer book.

(Marcia looks a touch nervous but gratified by these details. I offer them up, for what they are worth.)

She addressed the crowd who were gathered below her. She did her father proud, that much was certain, and he did not deserve a daughter so intelligent and kind. She was clearly innocent and everyone there knew it.

The axeman and I kept exchanging glances. He was used to seeing me on these rare state occasions, but he liked to take centre-stage. He was a true professional, a past master at the art of taking people's heads off. No bungler, him. I could tell at a glance.

His blade was polished and sharp, honed to a lethal gleam.

After kneeling in prayer, she took her off gloves and the handkerchief she had tied about her slender throat and gave them to Elizabeth Tilney. Then she passed her prayer book to the Lieutenant of the Tower.

The executioner stepped forward and went to untie her gown at the back, but she slapped him aside.

'I won't have you touch me yet. My ladies will oblige.'

She then allowed them to carefully undress her, the fastenings and ribbons, the pins, the headdress, until she stood only in her shift, a poor trembling thing, beautiful to behold.

(Marcia's eyes have begun to water.)

The man with the axe knelt and asked her forgiveness.

Marcia looks visibly moved by this detail but I add, 'It's a formality only. They always do it.' But I admit there was something heartfelt in the plea. He was a man of cold brute strength, but I had the feeling he did not relish this task much.

She was told to step forward. Piles of straw lay in front of her and scattered around the offending article – the block itself – in order to soak up the blood.

She looked down at it, and in that moment I felt her terror.

There it was, a wooden block with a dip carved out for the placing of the head. To lie there and wait for the blow, without moving, resisting the compulsion to leap away? How could that be borne? And by one so young, so full of energy and life?

('The readers will love this,' Marcia interjects softly.)

She turned to the man with the axe and said, 'I pray you dispatch me quickly.'

The blindfold was produced, but this seemed to distress Jane further.

'I cannot bear to be in darkness forever. Can I take it off before I lay me down?'

The executioner, having recovered some of his professional bearing, had become stern and remote once more. He refused.

By this time, her ladies were weeping. Elizabeth Tilney and Mistress Allan were in so much distress that they were unable to help at all. They had turned away, head in hands, unable to bear what was to follow. One of them appeared to faint.

Jane took the blindfold and tied it herself with trembling hands, but then a moment of panic followed.

'Where is it? I cannot see it! What am I to do?' she wailed, her arms held out before her like a cruel parody of blindman's bluff.

The sight on the scaffold was a sorry one by now. No one felt able to assist her. I stood amongst them, watching. No one could bear to help her lay her head down on that sinister block. She stumbled and almost fell, but then something strange happened.

There was a cry from below: someone broke away from the crowd and came bounding up the steps of the scaffold. No one stopped him. No one thought to try.

I've attended many hangings and beheadings, particularly of the notable and renowned, and never in all my days have I seen that happen before. Not at the Tower of London.

He took hold of her gently and led her forward, his arms wrapped around her in a gesture of kindness.

'Thank you,' I heard her say. He helped her to kneel and placed her hands for her, upon the block, so that they both found its shape together.

He then stood, this individual, an ordinary man of the people, and made to leave. But I noticed him scowl at the men gathered there – the executioner and the Lieutenant of the Tower. Without words, he shot them a look of barbed accusation. To do this? To a child?

Jane, meanwhile, placed her head in the curved aperture of the block and stretched out her body in one quick movement, with a single cry.

'Into thy hands I…'

The executioner was so quick she did not have time to finish her sentence.

No one touched the body until nightfall. She lay there, a little broken corpse without her head, throughout the long cold day, her blood seeping into the straw, dripping down through the gaps in the wooden platform.

I stood on the empty scaffold as the others left, and I listened to the wind, and I felt the pointlessness of what had been done, and Jane stood with me, to one side, a little puzzled perhaps.

She no longer felt the cold. She no longer felt the pain.

Marcia doesn't quite know what to say to this. She can hear that wind whistling through time, down the centuries, from that scaffold beneath the White Tower, to where we sit now, enthroned in our comfortable chairs, afternoon tea spread before us.

Painting in the Dark

There are good views from the hotel window here. I catch a glimpse of the Castle looming on top of its big black crag. I can recall the years before that castle was built. I can see a wild landscape, populated by bears and wolves, where the only 'buildings' were caves buried deep inside the belly of the rock.

I doubt Marcia will want to hear about that.

Those magical moments, prehistoric glimpses of wonder.

Those were the heady days of my early recruitment, when anything seemed possible, when it was interesting to see what humanity might become, what you might be capable of.

Thirty thousand years ago, I think, give or take.

A young girl standing on a rocky promontory, covered in ice which is in slow retreat. She surveys the land, her eyes scanning the horizon.

She can see me.

She acknowledges my presence with a faint movement of the head. Her courage intimidates me, fills me with awe.

She has climbed up a steep cliff-face, grabbing at footholds, a leather satchel strapped to her waist, made of deer-skin scraped with flint until soft and flexible. An undefined roaring in the distance, and trickling water from the snow-melt. There are multitudinous bird cries – such as you never hear now – fleets of them filling the air with their song. Animal sounds.

The Earth was thriving in its way, despite the death-grip of the ice. Life was being incubated beneath the glaciers which pushed their way across the land, grating rocks with their serrated edges, carving out mountains and valleys, scooping out hollows for the corries and magical lochans to be born in.

Inga, her name was.

The forest provided shelter, fuel and protection. At night, stars wheeled about the sky, a vast hemisphere of them. Glasgow, Edinburgh, all of it was covered with forest, dark, primeval corridors of giant trees, flourishing.

She lived with Nature. A different way of life. Light years away from Marcia with her painted fingernails and sculpted eyebrows.

Inga climbed, and when she had stopped climbing, she touched the stone surface before her. There were indentations, white circles and smooth cup marks. Inga ran her hands over them, gently exploring with her fingers, then she ducked down into the mouth of a cave.

I followed.

It swallowed us whole.

In the cave entrance she lit a small fire, taking flint from her satchel. She took out a small leather pouch of red powder, one of black, one of orange, and spread them on the floor – ochre, charcoal and blood – then a clutch of reeds. She stood up, and by the flaring light of her torch began to examine the wall of the cave, searching its dips and hollows, its jutting edges for the shapes she believed dwelt there. She ran her hands over the contours, then began to draw. She blew through the reed, spread red pigment in a fine powder, leaving a handprint on the rock. She took the end of the reed and the outline of a horse appeared beneath her quick deft movements, full of raw energy and power – she could see the creature in front of her, hear the stamp of its hooves, its breath exploding from its nostrils in an angry snort.

I watched in awe.

Truly, what this race of humans might be capable of is sublime, I told myself then.

Inga had been sent to perform this ritual for her tribe and she would return to them, having finished the task.

The cathedral of rock reared above us, its shadows immense, its walls alive with horses, buffalo, wolves. I could hear their cries echo as if they were in flight and in motion, hordes of them stampeding in the darkness. She used the shape and texture of the walls to release them from stone, endowing them with life.

When she had finished, she turned and looked directly at me.

She gathered up her few things, and together we began to descend the rock-face.

Her skill was not in question. She was an experienced climber. But a freezing wind began to blow. It brought shards of ice which stuck to her eyelashes and hair.

I respected her struggle, and felt her pain.

She hung onto the cliff-face, on a narrow ledge, like a little bird, and waited for the freezing wind to pass, but it brought snow, then more snow.

She glanced up at the mouth of the cave, far above. She had misjudged the weather. Simple as that. She ought to have stayed behind in the shelter of the cave, waited, but in her youth and haste, she was eager to get back to the others, tell them of her success, that she had completed it, a tribute to the gods, to ensure the hunt would continue for another year.

Now she curled up close against the rock and I sat with her, while her body slowly froze to ice. Night fell, and her spirit lifted and curled away from flesh and bone.

In the morning, when the sun rose, her body was stiff and grey, a statue etched into the cliff-face.

Brave Inga.

One of many.

I choose not to share this memory with Marcia. She wouldn't understand.

All that striving of humanity, that reaching for something sublime and ineffable... it promised so much.

And yet here we are...

Curtain!

Our interview has moved to a natural conclusion.

The iPhone sits between us on the low table and I long to scoop it up and listen to what she has recorded. I am greedy to know what she will include, how she will portray me.

As she slips the slender device into her bag, I take the liberty of asking her.

'I know it's a little premature, but do you have any idea, yet, what the interview will look like?'

She glances up at me, surprised.

'I'm just interested to know how you might portray me. Not that it matters, really.'

'Don't you worry,' she winks at me. 'You'll come out of it looking pretty good. A sympathetic portrayal is what we're after.'

I spare a thought for her readers, who might find the magazine lying there in a dentist's waiting room, or on the coffee table of a hair salon, and make the mistake of flipping through the glossy pages, caught by an awful fascination.

I like to think I have told my tale with pathos and humanity, with glimpses of humour and compassion, and that Marcia will comment favourably on this. I have opened up, given her a rare insight into the loneliness and isolation of my unique position. It hurts to be seen always as a pariah, an unwanted and unsought-for companion. No one wants to walk with Death.

Marcia raises a hand and the waiter is instantly at our side.

'The bill please!'

I risk a quick glance at him. Such pleasant young men nowadays, well-groomed, polite, ready to please, good at dealing with the general public, some of them. But a shard of ice enters my soul. *I know it... I can see it... what he cannot...*

A scooter in France, zipping along the back roads. He saved hard for that scooter, worked excessive overtime to pay for it, and the holiday.

I will meet him there, on that coastal road, at a blind bend where others have died before, a small shrine being testimony to the fact. I can already hear the screech of tyres, the smell of hot oil and warm leatherette, the stains in the dust, the back wheel spinning soundlessly. I will carry that young man in my arms, cradled like a baby, while the sun pours relentlessly from an empty blue sky.

He is back in an instant and Marcia slides her credit card on the plate, and leaves a generous tip.

It is with sorrow I watch him retreat across the reception room, a lightness in his step. I try not to think about the moment when we will meet again on that bend in the road.

That moment waits in his future as it waits in mine. As it waits for all of you.

'It must be so exhausting,' Marcia observes now, drawing the interview neatly to a close. 'I really don't know how you do it.'

'Oh, you know, one's work is everything, I suppose.'

'Thank you so much for taking time out of your busy schedule to meet me.'

'Not at all.'

'It was an absolute pleasure meeting you,' Marcia says.

'The pleasure is all mine.'

When this interview is over, I intend to make the most of the modern facilities upstairs. It's not often *Yours Truly* has time to unwind in five-star accommodation with a marble en suite, room service and a bar full of glittering cocktails. All courtesy of the bottomless expense account of *A Class Act Magazine*.

As Marcia walks away, I watch her carefully and sigh.

Such a pity, the way foreknowledge comes to me without warning, like a bolt from the blue.

I glance at my watch irritably. I have exactly fifty-five minutes to be prepared to greet Marcia on the other side. Cars race between the narrow canyons of the streets of Edinburgh nowadays, so unsuitable for modern road usage. Parking is a nightmare, I'm told, although I don't drive, of course. One of those swift metal chariots is waiting, even now, for our invincible Marcia Helen Sinclair.

One moment of distraction, a careless driver leaning towards the radio to adjust the station, coupled by coincidence with Marcia's own inattention, looking for her glasses in her bag, fearing she left them behind on the coffee table in the hotel.

Just at the moment she sees them there, safely ensconced in the shallows of its leathery interior... SLAM.

The moment of relief at finding her glasses will be followed by an eternity of oblivion.

Just like that, it happens, right when you were in the middle of doing something.

But I hadn't quite finished... I was watching that, I'm not quite...

Tough. No time for regrets or last chances. It's over. Curtain time.

No encore.

No last bow.

I barely have time to luxuriate in the tub, surrounded by a mountain of scented bubbles, candles and a Barbie-pink cocktail before I am summoned out once more.

The sun is still shining, oddly enough. When I get there, of course, it has already happened, or is in the process of happening. I kneel on the pavement beside Marcia where she was thrown, my hair still damp from the tub, hers covered in blood, and she opens her eyes. *Once. Twice.* Disbelief. Resignation. Humour.

Then she is gone.

I rise, and she rises beside me, and the two of us stand, ghost-like, on the pavement watching events unfold.

In the distance we hear sirens carving up the air.

'It might take them a while to arrive,' I tell her.

She nods.

'The Festival! Mad with tourists this time of year. Sorry,' I murmur.

She gives a light shrug, robbed of the power of speech at last, just when her career was going so well.

Later, when the paramedics have been and gone, and the driver of the vehicle has been interviewed by police and sits staring into space repeating, *'Sorry,'* and just occasionally, *'I don't like Classic FM, you see. Otherwise, I wouldn't have...'* and the street has been cleared of debris from the accident (which has been reported in the traffic news with a warning to avoid that area of town) I do the unthinkable.

I break the rules.

Something glitters in the gutter, its screen cracked. Marcia's iPhone.

I take it with me back to my five-star accommodation on Princes Street (all expenses paid), fetch my keys at reception, glide up in the elevator to my hermetically-sealed haven on the first-floor.

Ease into a chair, take out the iPhone.

It still works, surprisingly.

It's the work of a moment to find and locate our interview.

It pains me to know that after all this confession, all this opening up of the arteries and spilling of the beans, the world will never know, unless I manage to send the recorded evidence to the offices of *A Class Act Magazine*. In light of her sudden demise, will they still want to publish? Seems doubtful somehow.

It's unthinkable the interview should be wasted.

I try the camera app first, remembering how the kind waiter offered to take a photo of us.

As I suspected, snapshot after snapshot of Marcia standing alone, a blank space beside her, smiling and greeting thin air, talking to no one.

Despite all my best efforts, I am invisible.

A blank slate, and yet I carry so much.

Oh well, that was to be expected, I suppose.

Then I find and locate the recorded interview.

I hear Marcia's dulcet silvery tones emitted into the air of the hotel room from the half-crushed little device.

'It's so good of you to meet me like this, at such short notice,' she begins.

Then a gap – silence filled with static.

'I've taken the liberty of ordering afternoon tea for us both. I hope that meets with your approval? I don't know how much of an appetite you have, but...'

'Oh, yummy!' her voice says. 'Do help yourself. You must be half-starved.'

I had picked at the morsel on my plate, wishing I could share her enjoyment. My taste buds did not seem to oblige. Sometimes, on bad days, it's as if all I can taste is ash and sorrow. Other people's sorrow. It taints me, like a bad smell. There is no perfume in the world that can mask the scent of death. Blood, entrails, diesel fumes, decay, cordite, charcoal, rotting matter, metal, rank river water... and sometimes, on one or two occasions, lilies.

I struggle to remember the pattern of our interview, listening for my own voice.

'You don't have any allergies or anything? Vegan?'

I listen again, my ears straining.

'Do you mind if I...?'

Again, there is a slight pause. A staticky silence.

'There. Just ignore it.' A slight clank as she popped the phone onto the glass coffee table between us.

'So,' Marcia's voice again, a remnant of her living

self, left behind on this device until someone presses *delete*. 'The first thing our readers will want to know is…' I remember her gaze as it swept disparagingly over me, a trace of condescension, 'your sense of style. What you're wearing this season.'

I listen desperately for my own reply. Slide my finger along the cursor to fast forward.

Nothing. Just static. Static. Static.

Marcia's little device has failed to record a single word. At that moment, I feel indescribably lonely.

You people flower so fleetingly on this earth, before you leave with barely a backward glance. The next generation moves to replace you, likewise deluded into believing they too will live forever, their future extending into a glorious vanishing horizon of unending tomorrows.

Then the surprise comes.

Bang!

While I remain, dragging my burden along endless corridors of darkness.

But I shall let you into a secret.

I would rather be you, with your silly little lives full of brevity and beauty.

So brief.

So beautiful.

And what you will have at the end, I promise you, is this.

Tenderness and peace. Which go hand in hand with sorrow.

For me, that sense of peace will never come.

For you, it will.

Signing off, because there is nothing left to say, and no one left to hear it.

Yours Truly.

P.S. See you on the other side.

ACKNOWLEDGEMENTS

Thank you to all the usual suspects who offer support and encouragement, including family and friends, librarians, bookshops, book bloggers and reviewers, and of course readers - those who have supported me by reading my books and coming along to the launches. Also to schools, libraries and festival organisers throughout Scotland who have invited me over the years to give talks, and to the Scottish Book Trust for supporting all writers with their Live Literature Scheme. Clare at Fledgling deserves a special thank you. I really appreciate her unfailing confidence in liking my stuff and putting it out there. I am full of admiration for the way Fledgling will publish books that are different and original, and for Clare's courage and honesty in the way she socks it to the publishing world. Thank you to my brother and sister, Nick and Liz, for being so encouraging and making helpful noises, to my husband Joe for taking the flak when I'm in the doldrums (creatively speaking) and encouraging me to keep going. I feel very lucky in my children, Micah and Martha. I hugely appreciate their unfailing belief in the whole writing thing, absorbed through their DNA. I don't think I could have asked for more supportive or encouraging offspring. Big thanks to all of the above, and anyone not named.